Shandra Higheagle Mystery Books

Double Duplicity
Tarnished Remains
Deadly Aim
Murderous Secrets
Killer Descent
Reservation Revenge
Yuletide Slaying
Fatal Fall
Haunting Corpse
Artful Murder
Dangerous Dance
Homicide Hideaway
Toxic Trigger-point
Abstract Casualty
Capricious Demise
Vanishing Dream
A novella
Christmas Chaos

Deadly Aim

A Shandra Higheagle Mystery

Paty Jager

Windtree Press
Corvallis, Oregon

DEADLY AIM
Copyright © 2015 Patricia Jager

Contact Information: info@windtreepress.com
Windtree Press
Corvallis, OR
Visit us at http://windtreepress.com

Cover Art by Covers by Karen
Photograhy by: Paty Jager amd Deposit Photos

Published in the United States of America
ISBN 9781940064963

Dedication

Thank you to Maggie Holcomb, Angie Conner, Lauri Robinson, and Danita Cahill. Without your insights and expertise to make my writing sparkle, this journey I've embarked on wouldn't be possible.

Chapter One

After a two-week sojourn of teaching and displaying her pottery at an art show in New Mexico, Shandra Higheagle needed this leisurely horseback ride to get back in tune with nature. She breathed deep, inhaling the pine scent and undertones of decaying plant life. The changing colors and brisk autumn air energized Shandra.

Lil, Shandra's Jill-of-all-trades, had suggested the ride. Every time Shandra spent more than a few days off the mountain she had to get reacquainted with her roots in order to re-submerge herself in her art.

Her bear-sized dog, Sheba, loped ahead disappearing through the huckleberry bushes. The dog loved lumbering over Huckleberry Mountain while Shandra rode her horse.

It wasn't just her time away that had Shandra's mind wandering. Only one week and she'd be attending Ryan's brother's wedding to Ryan's ex-girlfriend. Shandra and the handsome Weippe detective hadn't made any kind of commitment to one another, but she did find his company pleasurable. And she had to admit, she was curious about his family and the woman who he'd set his sights on marrying in seventh grade.

"Woof! Woof!"

Sheba's excited bark caught Shandra's attention. It didn't sound like her pursuing or scared bark. It had a mournful lilt to it.

"Where are you girl?" Shandra stood in the stirrups and scanned the area she'd last seen her dog. Her gelding, Apple, started dancing nervously and blew air in short snorts. Something had both animals on alert.

"Woof! Woof!"

She zeroed in on the sound and reined Apple that direction. Sheba's head was down and the way her body shook, she was digging.

"What is it girl?" Shandra dodged a tree limb as Apple snorted and started to back up.

"Whoa. What has you spooked?" She ran a hand down the horse's neck to soothe him and stared at the ground where Sheba pawed.

Her stomach lurched and her mouth went dry. Sheba dug at the ground next to a bloody, disemboweled body.

Apple pivoted with barely a touch of the reins. Shandra sat with her back to the sight. Bile rose in her throat. She usually wasn't squeamish, but this was the first time she'd witnessed a mauled human. "Sheba, come!" she ordered without glancing back. When Sheba appeared beside the horse, Shandra leaned down and patted the dog on the head. "Good girl. Stay."

She straightened in the saddle and the image flashed in her mind. "Why do I find all the bodies on this mountain?" This body didn't capture her imagination like the thirty-year-old bones she'd found in her clay pocket. She shivered and searched the forest around her. Nothing lurked but she couldn't shake the fear prickling her skin.

The small bar on her phone faded in and out. "I have to give it a try. I don't want to leave this poor person to any more animals." She found Ryan's name and pushed the dial button. "Not again. Ryan's not going to believe this anymore than I do."

"Shandra, I…thinking…you."

His voice cutting in and out wasn't a good sign.

"I found a body. Go to my ranch and have Lil bring you out to me." She hoped he heard enough to know what to do.

"Body? Are… How…" The connection broke.

Drawing a deep breath, Shandra tried to decide how to keep the body safe from any more animals. She couldn't leave Sheba. The dog's size would be daunting for most animals, but if an animal so much as growled, Sheba would dash back to the ranch faster than a jet.

Her phone beeped.

Glancing at the front, she spotted a text message.

Where R you? Ryan asked.

She typed back. *Found body along east property line. Lil can bring you.*

K, he texted in reply.

Now, to spend two hours waiting for them without looking at the body. Who could this be and why were they on my property? She tied Apple to a tree, sat down on a log, and hugged Sheba. "I've never felt scared on the mountain before."

~*~

Ryan was a half hour from Huckleberry and then another forty-five minutes from Shandra's ranch. He was beginning to think the woman was a body detector. First the gallery owner, then the thirty-year-old skeleton, and who knew what she'd stumbled across this time. The only thing he did know—he'd always be there for the eccentric artist. The past few months he'd spent more and more time with the woman. The more he learned about her, the more he knew she was the one. When he could shed his demons and settle down, he'd ask her to marry him.

With lights flashing and sirens blaring, he swerved off Hwy 90, turned right, and barreled down the main street of Huckleberry. The ritzy resort had been off-limits to a sheep rancher's son growing up forty miles away, but now it was part of his territory as a Weippe County Detective.

No sooner had he entered and exited town than he was flying at eighty miles an hour up the county road toward Shandra's ranch. The woman liked living on her mountain. The more he visited her there, the more he understood how the area revitalized and fed her artistic talents. Part of his speed was to find the body, but the other part was the fact Shandra had been gone for two weeks. He'd told himself he'd give her a couple days to recuperate then invite himself to dinner. He'd never planned on seeing her again because of a dead body.

He whipped his SUV up a side road nearly hidden by overgrown pines. This bumpy, miserable excuse for a road was Shandra's way of keeping people out. It looked like a forest service road and wasn't vehicle friendly. He had to slow the Tahoe to a crawl to navigate the bumps and not toss all his equipment in the back into a heap. The house, studio, and barn came into view and he understood Shandra's penchant for not wanting to leave her place.

His siren was still blaring. Lil, Shandra's employee, walked out of the barn with the old orange cat wrapped around her neck like a live fur stole. The woman wore her signature purple clothing. Today it was an over-sized sweatshirt and stocking cap. Her gray hair stuck out like spikes on a flail.

He braked in front of the barn, shut off the lights and siren, and hopped out of the vehicle. "Shandra called. She's found another body."

Lil shook her head. "What is with that woman?"

"My thoughts exactly." Ryan strode toward the barn with Lil beside him. "She said it was along the east property line and you'd know how to get me there."

Lil nodded and pointed to the gelding Ryan used when he and Shandra trail rode together.

He walked to the stall. "Hey, Duke. We're after another body, you game?" He led the horse out and had him saddled by the time Lil swung up into the saddle of her horse.

"Is the east property line very far?" He wondered about logistics to get the coroner and other deputies to the site.

"About an hour. If she said I knew where she was, then she's on her usual route for a trail ride." Lil nudged her horse, and they trotted into the trees.

I might as well gather information. "Who owns the land bordering Shandra's on the east?"

"J.W. Randal."

He wished he could pull out his notebook and jot that down, but the trail so far was fairly smooth and Lil kept the gait at a trot.

"Full-time land owner or a seasonal resident?"

"Full-time."

Lil was always one for few words, but he'd like some elaboration. "What does he use the land for?"

Lil slowed her horse and stared at him. "Cattle and big game hunting."

She said the last with contempt.

"He has the required license to do big game hunts?" Randal. The name was familiar. Where had he heard it? He'd tried to learn all the licensed big game hunting reserves.

"All I know is people pay lots of money to shoot animals on his place. He was in the paper a few weeks ago for using illegal tags."

Chapter Two

Shandra sat on a log, her back to the body. Her arms were wrapped around Sheba's neck. She'd tried everything she could think of to console the dog, but Sheba wouldn't stop whimpering.

"It's okay, girl. There's nothing we can do for that person except help Ryan find out what happened."

Apple raised his head and nickered. A reply muffled by the thick fir and pine trees was followed by the thump of horse's hooves. Lil and Ryan.

Shandra stood, waiting for their approach. She shouldn't be excited to see Ryan given the circumstances, but during her two weeks away, she'd thought of the man every moment she wasn't teaching or talking to art gallery owners. Even Professor Landers, who'd ruined her faith in love and men, had never been on her mind as much as the Weippe detective.

Lil appeared out of the trees first. The woman's

gaze peered into Shandra. They'd become closer since Lil had been a suspect for the murder of the last body Shandra had found. She knew her employee cared as much about her as she did about her reclusive employee.

When Ryan appeared, Shandra's gaze leapt to the man. His dark eyes crinkled at the edges as his wide mouth tipped up into an inviting smile. His square chin and jawline was the right combination of masculinity. Because of her artistic nature she'd always been drawn to men whose faces could be chiseled from stone.

Her gaze didn't leave Ryan as he dismounted and walked up to her.

"I was anxious to see you, but this isn't the way I'd wanted our first meeting after your trip."

She smiled at his joking tone. "Me either."

"Did you find more bones?" Lil asked, breaking the silence that had lapsed while Shandra stared at Ryan.

"No. This body was alive not that long ago, I think." She swallowed. "The animals have been feasting."

Ryan's face sobered. He slipped the pack on his back to the ground and pulled out a camera. "Where's the body?"

Shandra pointed to the area behind her.

Ryan's gaze followed her pointing finger. "You two stay here. I'll assess the situation."

He disappeared behind the trees. Shandra faced Lil. "Do you know the man who owns the land next door?"

"J.W. Randal."

Shandra stared at Lil. "The man everyone was talking about before I left?" Her mind ran back over the heated conversations she'd eavesdropped on at Ruthie's café on her last trip to town before heading to Arizona.

"Yep. He's been getting all types of people riled up since you left. Mostly his wife. I heard her screaming at him outside the bank. His illegal hunts are costing them lots in fines." Lil grinned. "After the one was discovered, they started digging into J.W.'s finances."

A shiver slithered down Shandra's back. "Do you think that's J.W. over there?"

Lil shrugged. "It could be a lost hiker or a hunting accident."

Shandra had a feeling the mutilated body Ryan was snapping photos of was her neighbor and that he hadn't had an accident.

~*~

Ryan stepped around the trees and stared down at the bloody, torn body. Hell of a way for a man to die. He hoped the poor guy was dead before the animals made a snack of him. He snapped photos as his mind took in the wounds, the clothing, and the lack of hunting or hiking gear. Studying the ground around the corpse, he spotted the direction the body had been dragged.

He took photos of the drag marks, donned a glove, and slid his hand under the body, feeling for a wallet and identification. Nothing. It was odd that a person out in the woods wouldn't be carrying any identification. Unless it was back at his camp. He peered at the drag marks and made his decision.

Ryan returned to the two women. Seeing Shandra when he rode out of the trees had tumbled his heart. He knew something had happened in her past that she wasn't ready to reveal to him. The experience kept her heart at a distance. He was willing to take the time to break through that barrier.

"Did you find out who it is?" Shandra asked, walking toward him.

"There wasn't any identification, and the animals have ruined any facial recognition."

Shandra's head bobbed, and Lil's face paled.

"Lil, ride back to the ranch and call the sheriff's department. Tell them a body was found on this property. I'm keeping an eye on it and to send deputies and the coroner." He nodded to the horses. "You'll have to bring everyone up here. Take the horses with you."

"What about you and Shandra?" Lil's gaze traveled from her employer to him and back to her employer.

"We'll be fine. Ryan has a gun." Shandra smiled.

"But if there are dangerous animals out here…" Lil let the thought trail off.

"We'll have Sheba," Shandra said.

Both Lil and Ryan burst out laughing.

Ryan had been scared of the large dog the first time they'd met, but he'd learned quickly the dog was all bark and trepidation.

"Okay," Shandra grinned. "Sheba won't protect us, but her size does keep most of the wild animals from getting too close."

"We'll be fine." Ryan said, gathering the reins to his horse and Shandra's. "But you might tell them to hurry to get in and out before dark."

Lil nodded and mounted her horse.

Ryan stood beside Shandra watching the last of the horse's rumps disappear in the trees.

She faced him. "How are we going to spend the

next several hours?"

The glint in her eyes shouldn't have yanked his mind from his work, but it did. He gently drew her closer and settled his lips over hers. He'd missed their sweetness seconds after he'd kissed her good-bye before she headed to Arizona.

Slowly, he pulled out of the kiss. "How did your trip go?"

"Hmmm…" Her eyelids were closed. Her dark lashes fanned out over her high, tanned cheek bones.

His gaze lingered on her pink lips. He wanted to kiss her again, but there was work to do. He tapped her perfect-sized nose, making her eyelids flip open, giving him the pleasure of gazing into her golden eyes.

"Tell me about your trip while we follow the drag marks." He captured her hand. He liked she didn't have soft palms. They were rough and slightly calloused from working with clay.

Her grip pulled him to a stop. "I don't have to look at the body again do I?"

He couldn't stop the smile tipping at the corners of his mouth. "No." He tugged on her hand, leading her to the far side of the body.

"See how those plants are smashed and bent." He pulled a flashlight out of the backpack slung over his shoulder. "And those dark spots. That's blood." Ryan glanced at Shandra. "Let's see if we can find out where this body came from."

"Are you sure we should leave the it? What if more animals come back?"

"We won't be gone long. Hold the flashlight, please." Ryan pulled the camera out of his bag and snapped photos every five yards. Their path was blocked by a four strand barbwire fence.

"This is the property line." Shandra stated.

Sheba sniffed the bottom wire and whimpered.

Ryan crouched down. "Shine the light on this wire."

As he'd expected. Dried blood. "Whatever dragged the body, took it under the fence." He studied the ground on the other side. An area larger than the body was smashed and trampled.

"What are you staring at?" Shandra asked.

"I'm not sure."

Chapter Three

Shandra enjoyed watching Ryan study and decipher the information he found. Right now he was staring at the smashed-down vegetation on the other side of the fence.

"Could the animals have attacked him here?" she asked.

Ryan shook his head. "There should be more blood if several animals were dining on him in this spot."

Shandra's stomach roiled at the thought. She stared at the grass and tried not to envision wolves or cougars attacking the man.

"Ladies first." Ryan held two of the strands of wire wide apart.

She ducked through and held the wire for him to step through. Sheba whimpered on the other side. Knowing the dog would be scared standing alone by the fence, Shandra put a foot on the bottom wire shoving it down and held the next wire up. Sheba ducked her head and dropped her back to make it through the opening. She licked Shandra's hand in thank you.

"You're welcome." Shandra patted the dog's head. She wouldn't want to be left alone out here either, knowing there was a dead body.

"This doesn't make sense." Ryan crouched at the edge of the area that was disturbed.

"What?"

"There aren't any paw prints in this bit of dirt. See how the plant is bent like something stepped on it? There should be at least nail indentions if the animal was dragging and digging its paws into the ground to pull the body." Ryan took photos of the area.

Shandra watched. His camera flashed and something sparkled on the ground. "Flash again," she said, this time staring at the area the sparkle had caught her attention.

Ryan took another photo. She pinpointed the object and knelt. Moving her hands over the plants, she felt something that wasn't a rock. It was a small, blue crystal, flower pendant. She sat back on her haunches and stared at Ryan.

"Either our body was playing both ways or there was a woman out here." She held the flower out to Ryan.

"You shouldn't have touched that." He pulled out a small plastic bag.

She dropped the pendant in the bag. "This could be a clue."

"It could. And now it has your prints on it."

"Sorry, I didn't think about that. I knew it shouldn't be here and had to be a clue." She was sorry. She didn't need to be connected to another death as a suspect. The first time she was a suspect she'd let her mother's paranoia make her defensive.

He tucked the little bag away in his backpack and stood. "Let's follow this a little farther in."

Shandra grasped Sheba's collar and followed behind Ryan. She studied every spot he stopped and took a photo. The bent plants and drag marks took them another fifty yards into her neighbor's property. She'd never met Mr. Randal, but his wife had purchased one of her vases at the local art event last year. The woman had been friendly and seemed to like living up on the mountain as much as Shandra did.

Ryan stopped abruptly. Shandra stalled her feet in time to keep from slamming her head into his back.

"What did you find?" She moved to step around him.

Ryan put out an arm. "You don't want to see this."

Fear trickled down her backbone like a slithering ice cube. "Why? Is it another body?"

"Not human. Looks like someone shot an elk and only took the horns. But the body has been partially eaten."

Ryan's camera clicked.

Shandra remained where she was, facing back the way they'd come. "What kind of animals would eat an elk and a man?" she asked, shivering at the thought she'd rode her horse alone over this mountain hundreds of times since purchasing it. Were the mountain lions and bears always this aggressive?

Ryan reappeared. "It's not just one animal. There are mountain lions, bears, wolves, coyotes, and the birds who all eat meat and will lunch on anything they find. An already dead creature is an easy meal."

Wings flapped and the limbs of the pine tree they stood under rustled. Shandra looked up. Three turkey vultures peered down at her with ugly, red, bald heads and large beady eyes. Even knowing it was all part of a food chain didn't stop the shudder vibrating through her. She knew from a story told to her the summer Shandra stayed with her grandmother, that buzzards were an omen of danger.

Ryan put a hand on the lower part of Shandra's back and urged her to walk. "Let's go back to the body. It's going to take search and rescue efforts to scour this ground for clues." He didn't like the fact they'd found an elk stripped of what was most likely a trophy rack. The man on Shandra's property could have wandered across a poacher's path or even been trying to catch them. If there were poachers on this mountain it made the whole forest unsafe. He wanted Shandra back at her ranch. Poachers were illegal hunters and had no scruples.

"We didn't find his camp or where he might have come from?" Shandra said, stopping and turning to confront him.

"I believe we found the point of confrontation. Once I gather evidence, I'm pretty sure the forensic lab will find our victim's blood mixed in with that of the elk."

Her eyes widened. "You think he was killed over the elk?"

Ryan nodded and started her moving again.

She kept walking, but asked, "I've heard of poachers killing animals and only taking horns. Is that what you think? The man came upon poachers?"

"Yes." He wasn't going to elaborate and scare her.

They arrived at the fence.

Shandra faced him. "Do you think they are crossing the fence to my property?"

He shrugged. "With poachers you never know."

Her eyes flashed and her facial features hardened like a stone statue. "The creatures on my property aren't fair game for poachers. I'll hire someone to ride the fence line and check for interlopers."

Ryan held the wire on the fence for her. "As long as it isn't you riding the fence alone."

Her expression softened. "I'm an artist, not a lawman. I know my strengths. Riding a fence line like a border patrol officer isn't one of them."

"I'm glad to hear you know your boundaries." Ryan slipped through the wire Shandra held for him. He stepped on the bottom wire and called Sheba through.

"Now what do we do until Lil gets back with the others?" Shandra strolled to the uphill side of where the body lay.

Ryan heard squawking in the vicinity of the body. "Stay here," he said and hurried to the crime scene. Several turkey vultures squabbled over the body. Ryan hurried forward waving his arms. "Go on! Get!"

Once the birds were out of sight he called to Shandra. "Looks like I'll be shooing away hungry critters."

Chapter Four

Shandra sat with her back against Ryan's on a large granite rock. He faced the body, and she stared into the forest with Sheba resting her head on her lap. Ryan had yelled and waved his arms about ten times while they sat propped against one another.

"Is this the first time you've had to secure a crime scene by keeping birds and animals away?" She didn't want to think about the body, but it was hard to forget it existed when Ryan kept shooing animals away.

"In Chicago I had a similar situation, only it was in the streets and it was a wealthy man. Had to keep the homeless from taking the body's clothes."

His monotone delivery hid his true feelings about the incident.

"Did you like being a policeman in the city?" She felt his back stiffen.

"No."

"Why did—"

Sheba barked a welcome and Lil's horse appeared through the trees. She led Apple and Duke. It appeared the deputies had brought their own horses. Behind her was Dr. Porter, the local doctor and coroner, riding Sammy. Behind him rode Maxwell Treat, son of the local mortician and a search and rescue member. He rode his large horse, Zeus, and led a pack horse. Behind him were two deputy sheriffs mounted on their own horses.

Where Dr. Porter could be mistaken for an albino, his hair and skin were so pale, Maxwell was the complete opposite with shiny black curls and dark mahogany skin. And while the doctor was average size, though on the thin side, Maxwell stood a good six-and-a-half feet with shoulders so broad she'd witnessed him walk sideways to get through some of the doors in Huckleberry.

Ryan stood and met the group before they came any closer. "Good to see you, Doc. Treat. The body is on the other side of Ms. Higheagle." He turned to the deputies. "Ms. Higheagle found the body while riding." Ryan moved the dismounted deputies a little farther away and talked in a quiet manner not allowing his voice to carry.

Shandra stood by the rock and waited for Dr. Porter and Maxwell to reach her. "It's not pretty to look at."

"No dead body is," Maxwell said, a big grin on his face.

"This one has been partially eaten," she said, thinking the men needed to be told what to expect.

Dr. Porter looked over her shoulder, cringed, and

his pale complexion became even more pasty white. "From here, I pronounce the man dead." He plopped onto her rock and pulled papers out of the old-fashioned doctor's bag he'd untied from the saddle horn.

Maxwell's expression became serious. "Who is it?" he asked.

"I don't know. Ryan didn't find any identification." She smiled up at the man staring at the body. "Ryan said something about getting a search and rescue party together. You going to join in?" Maxwell had been part of the party that excavated the skeleton she'd found over a month ago.

"I can't this time. Pop's going on vacation. I have to be at the mortuary." Disappointment rang in his voice.

Ryan approached with the two deputies. "Shandra, you and Lil can ride back to your place. We'll be here a while and may need you to guide more officers into the area."

Shandra knew he was getting her away on purpose, but she didn't care. She'd do some digging into her neighbor from the safety of her couch.

"I'm happy to get out of here." She walked over to Lil and the horses. Glancing over her shoulder, she found Maxwell and the officers all huddled together.

Dr. Porter walked briskly toward the horses. "There's no more need for me anymore. I'll ride back with you ladies."

Shandra hid the smile twitching at her lips. She'd discovered a bit about Dr. Maynard Porter's history. He grew up in the city, and while he had the credentials and abilities to be practicing at a major hospital, he was stuck in Huckleberry taking care of an ailing great aunt until she died. It had been a codicil to his uncle's will. If he didn't take care of his aunt, he didn't inherit his great grandfather's recreational property. She'd also learned that the property meant more to Dr. Porter than its monetary value. He'd spent many winters and summers at the place.

Dr. Porter mounted Sammy, the chestnut gelding she used for packing the clay down the mountain.

Shandra made sure the horses Maxwell and the deputies rode were tied, and she left Duke for Ryan. If other officers were called in, she hoped they brought their own horses. She didn't have enough to supply the whole Weippe sheriff's department.

She swung up on Apple, whistled for Sheba, and followed Lil back home. No reason not to start questioning the doctor who moved in the same circles as her neighbor.

"Dr. Porter, do you know J.W. Randal?" Shandra asked, holding her horse to a walk beside Sammy.

The doctor peered into her eyes a moment before clearing his throat. "You want the truth or do you want me to be diplomatic?"

Aha, her neighbor had dirt. "The truth."

"He's a pompous ass."

Shandra laughed. "Please, don't hold back."

Dr. Porter grinned. "I'm not supposed to talk bad about my patients but J.W. isn't my patient. His wife, however, is my patient. I don't know how the woman puts up with him."

She latched onto the last little tidbit. "Is he abusive?"

"No, not physically, that I know of. But I've

witnessed him verbally lambast her at a public function." He shook his head. "Not something anyone wants to witness or be the recipient of, I'm sure."

"Do they have children?"

"No, but Vivian's niece lives with them. Cecily Wagner. She's in her last year of high school." Dr. Porter narrowed his eyes. "Why are you so interested in J.W. and his family?"

"Detective Greer and I followed the drag marks while waiting for the rest of you. The body was killed on the Randal property."

~*~

Ryan filled Deputies Gerald Speaks and Ron Trapp in on what he and Shandra discovered while retracing the drag marks. "The best way to figure out what happened would be to do a thorough search and gather as much evidence as we can."

Gerald nodded. "Once the body is gone we can bring in the search and rescue. Have them comb the forest for clues."

"Do you have any idea who the body is?" Ron asked.

"Not until the autopsy is done or we find someone in missing persons who resembles the description." Ryan noted Treat had the body bagged and ready to place on the pack horse he'd brought with him.

He walked over and helped place the body on the horse. "I'll ride back with you and the body. I want to find out who this is. It will help to discover why he was out here."

"I'll be ready to hit the trail soon as I tie him on." Treat looped a thin rope through special metal rings on the pack saddle, lacing it back and forth over the body.

Ryan walked back to where the two deputies placed pieces of evidence in plastic bags. "I'll head out with the body and start making missing person inquiries. I'll send in more help."

"As long as you leave our horses, we'll be fine. I'd hate to have to walk out of here," Gerald said.

"Yes, why would someone be hiking on private property, unless…" Ryan had some calls to make once he had better cell reception.

He mounted Duke and rode alongside Treat as long as the trail remained wide enough. "What can you tell me about the neighbors on the east side of Shandra's property?"

Treat shook his head slowly. "J.W. was pulled in for selling illegal hunting tags to the people who paid to hunt on his property."

"Pulled in? As in arrested?" How did he miss this information? Was that why the name had sounded familiar? He read or heard about it in passing?

"Yep. Big legal battle going on. He's trying to fight it even though he was caught red-handed by Melvin Clower of the Fish and Game." Treat's smile turned grim. "Melvin is a good man. Family man who cares about our forests and animals. If he says he caught J.W. doing illegal hunting, I believe him."

"Is Clower a local?" It appeared staying close to Huckleberry and digging up information would be a better way to spend his time once he placed the body in a wagon headed to the forensic lab.

Chapter Five

Shandra found Dr. Porter's information about her neighbor interesting. What she'd learned only fueled her need to discover more.

At the barn, Dr. Porter said good-bye and drove away in his BMW SUV. Shandra helped Lil unsaddle the horses and headed to the house.

"Aren't you going to work in the studio today?" Lil called.

Shandra spun around and nearly collided with Sheba. "No. It's late. After finding the body, I'm not feeling the least bit creative." She ruffled Sheba's fluffy ears. "Come on girl, we need to celebrate life after what we saw."

They entered the house through the back door. Shandra headed straight for the refrigerator. Nothing celebrated life like a caramel sundae. She made one for herself and one for Sheba. After placing one on the floor, she carried the other to the dining room.

At the table, she flipped open her laptop and started googling J.W. Randal, Weippe County, Idaho. It appeared he came from money, enjoyed making more, and believed himself above the law. The photos of him didn't help her determine if the mauled body was his. She'd barely looked at the corpse. Having the images of a mauled body in her mind wasn't good for her creative soul.

There were photos of his wife, mostly without J.W. "What kind of a marriage do they have? Maybe the body is Vivian's lover?" She continued browsing the information and studying the photos.

Sheba's barking startled her. "Who's out there, girl?"

Shandra flipped the computer monitor down and followed the sound of Sheba's excited barking.

She opened the door. Sheba shot out like a thoroughbred at the Kentucky Derby. Shandra watched Sheba's cumbersome lope and spotted two horses with riders and a pack horse.

Ryan and Maxwell dismounted near one of the horse trailers. They talked a moment before Ryan led Duke toward the barn.

Shandra hurried into the barn. "Where are the other two?"

"They started investigating. I need to discover who the body was." He unsaddled Duke and put him in the corral.

"From what Dr. Porter told me, I think the body is either J.W. Randal or was put there by him"

Ryan stared at her. "I know you like to stick your nose into homicides, but we don't even know that this man didn't die of natural causes."

Shandra crossed her arms. She hadn't planned on Ryan stonewalling her. After all, they'd riddled out murderers twice before. "If you think this is only an accident why did you leave two deputies on the mountain?"

He walked out of the barn. "We have to investigate and find the cause of death. Even if it is natural or accidental." Ryan stopped at his vehicle. "Stay out of this Shandra. And stay off the mountain until we've discovered the cause of death."

"And ruled out poachers?" she asked, knowing that was the reason he wanted her to stay off the mountain.

Ryan opened the door of his SUV and rolled the window down. "Yes, I want you to stay off the mountain in case it was poachers. They will shoot anyone they think could turn them in." He slid onto the driver's seat.

She cringed as her glimpse of the body flickered in the back of her mind. "Will there be more people to guide to the site?" Shandra didn't plan to go anywhere on the mountain alone until they discovered what had happened.

"I'm requesting a search party to comb the area we walked for evidence. They'll have their own horses, but Lil should lead them in."

Shandra smiled. "Lil? What if I want to go back up there?"

Ryan tipped his lips in a wry smile. "You won't just lead them up. You'll mess with evidence and get yourself tangled up in the investigation."

"And I thought it was because you didn't want me up on the mountain with the poachers." Shandra spun from the open window. "Let me know who I found," she said over her shoulder as she headed back to the house.

Ryan laughed at Shandra's departure. He knew there was no way the inquisitive woman could stay out of the investigation. Not only because the body was found on her property by her, but because she seemed to thrive on digging up clues to right wrongs.

He started his vehicle and drove down the mountain to Huckleberry. The small community would know if a local was missing, and the resort and hotels would be able to tell him if a patron hadn't returned. There were other factors that could keep the identity of the body hidden from them for a while. Lack of fingerprints or DNA in the system. No family that missed him. He could be homeless. So many unknowns.

The four parking slots allotted to the Huckleberry city police were empty. He'd also noted the streets didn't host as many people roaming about. The summer tourist season was waning. It would be a couple months until the skiers arrived by the droves.

Inside the police station, Hazel, a retired county clerk, manned the telephone and radio.

"You're starting to become a regular here. May need to ask Chief Marlow to set you up a desk." She smiled and answered the ringing phone.

Ryan waved and sat in the chair behind Officer Blane's desk. The rookie cop had been overzealous several months earlier when he'd cuffed Shandra after finding her with a dead body.

Ryan pulled up county-wide missing persons

reports. None matched the build of the body Shandra found. He spread his net wider, sifting through missing person records of the counties and then the states around them.

The front door opened and Blane charged over to the desk. "Why do you always use my desk?"

Ryan glared up at the rookie. "Do you see another computer that is hooked up to all the agencies?"

"You could use the chief's." He backpedaled. "Or the one where Hazel and Millie sit."

"Those are all being used." Ryan clicked out of the site he was in and stood. "I'm finished."

He sauntered up to Hazel's desk. "Need a cup of coffee?"

She winked. "Blane watch the radio and phone, I'll be back in fifteen."

Ryan followed the woman, who had to be past seventy, as she practically skipped to the break room. He'd used her local knowledge about people before and was confident she could help him with this case.

Hazel poured two cups of coffee and sat at the table. Ryan took a seat across from her and sipped his coffee.

"This have anything to do with the body that Higheagle lady found on her property." She frowned. "That young lady seems to find a lot of bodies."

Ryan nodded. "Unfortunately there wasn't much she could do about the last two. Huckleberry Mountain has been a favorite place for leaving bodies for years." He remembered a big scandal that happened when he was a boy and the resort was just becoming popular. A benefactor of the resort had gone missing and the body never found. Though speculation was he had gone skiing and fell into a crevasse. There were still a few who thought he was murdered because of a feud going on between him and the locals.

Hazel bobbed her gray curls. "This mountain has some rugged terrain. This body, was it an accident?"

"We won't know until forensics takes a look at him."

Her fading green eyes widened. "You know who it is?"

"Only that he's male. The animals made facial recognition useless."

She cringed. "Bet that wasn't something that artist liked seeing."

"No. It wasn't pleasant for anyone to see." Ryan swallowed half the cup of coffee, thankful it was Hazel's brew and not the chief's. His coffee went down like battery acid.

"Why'd you ask me to have coffee?" Hazel peered at him over her cup.

"What can you tell me about the Randals?"

"You think it was J.W.?" Hazel's crooked smile revealed she tried to hide a gleeful smirk.

Ryan jumped on the obvious. "Is J.W. Randal a likable man?"

Hazel shook her head and narrowed her eyes. "I doubt you'll find a person in Huckleberry who likes the man, including his wife."

Chapter Six

"Why's that?" Ryan asked, taking a sip of his coffee and watching Hazel closely. So far the woman had shown little bias when he'd asked her about locals. Something about J.W. Randal dug in her craw.

"You can ask anyone in the community, they'll all tell you the same. When a man has no respect for the law—government or nature, he is the lowest."

"Are you talking about the charges brought up against him for illegal use of hunting tags?" Ryan had looked the allegations up on the computer while he was online.

"That and the way he treats people and animals." She leaned closer. "I heard him tell his wife if she wasn't an iceberg in bed, he wouldn't have to look elsewhere." She leaned back, her eyes wide behind wireless glasses. "This was in the middle of a charity event. J.W. was standing with his arm around the shoulders of a young, and I mean young, woman.

Vivian didn't say anything to him, and he blurted that tidbit loud enough for half the crowd to hear."

"What would Vivian get if J.W. was dead?" The wife sounded like a good suspect if the body turned out to be Randal.

"I doubt she'd get anything. From what I've heard, his illegal hunting has nearly wiped them out with legal fees and fines." Hazel picked up her coffee cup. "I've never seen Vivian stand up to J.W. It would take a pretty strong backbone of courage to kill a person, I'd think. And she has just as much money as J.W." She stood. "I need to get back to my desk. Blane messes up everything."

Ryan looked at his watch. If he headed to Warner, the county seat and where he had a small apartment, he could pack a bag and be back in the area by ten. He'd book a room on the way out of town. If he kept catching homicides in the Huckleberry area he might have to start working out of here instead of Warner.

~*~

Shandra spent the better part of the evening scanning the internet for information about J.W. Randal and his family. What she didn't understand was why a man who appeared to be a savvy businessman, would start up an illegal hunting reserve on his property.

"Had his hubris become so big he thought he could get away with illegal hunting?" She scratched Sheba's head and shut the computer screen. Her eyes stung, and she'd been stifling yawns the last half hour. "Let's go to bed."

She carried her sundae bowl into the kitchen, turned out the lights, and headed to her room. In bed, she turned off the lights. The minute she closed her eyes the mauled body spun in her head.

Clicking on the bedside lamp, she fluffed the pillows, and sat against the carved headboard. "Come here." She beckoned Sheba, patting the bed beside her. Always an eager bed partner, Sheba crawled from the foot of the bed to lay alongside Shandra.

"You might be scared of your own shadow, but having you here makes me feel safe." She wrapped an arm around the fluffy neck and leaned her cheek on the furry head. Slowly her eyelids closed as she snuggled with her furry talisman.

Shandra walked through the forest, looking right and left and jumping at each sound. Ella appeared. "Do not fear the mountain. It did no wrong."

"I saw the body. It was…" A shiver slithered down her spine..

Ella wrapped her arms around Shandra. "The animals must eat to survive. They do not ask to be hunted. They are not the killers."

"Is my mountain safe?" Shandra stared into the brown eyes she'd grown fond of too late.

"You will come to no harm." Ella disappeared, taking with her Shandra's fear.

Shandra woke. She smiled at the dream and turned the light off. Tomorrow Ryan should know who the person was, and I'll go to the mountain and look for clues to his death.

~*~

Ryan blinked at the phone buzzing and vibrating on the bedside table. His eyes focused and he swiped a finger across the screen.

"Detective Greer, this is Sheila Rickman at the

Forensic lab. I have an identification on that body you sent in yesterday." The matter-of-fact female voice pulled him completely awake.

"Did you also determine cause of death?" He leaned over to grab his shirt from the chair and dug for his note pad in the pocket.

"Yes. John Wayne Randal was shot once through the heart."

Ryan whistled. "One shot in the heart. That is either luck or premeditated to have that kind of aim."

"He also had traces of hair, blood, and bone of the cervus canadensis under his fingernails."

"Is that a plant?"

"No, Rocky Mountain Elk."

Ryan sat up straighter. "He was the one who killed the elk and took the horns." But where were the horns? And who shot him? Did he have an accomplice?

"I'll send the full report to you in an email." Her clipped tone proved she had more to do than talk on the phone.

"Thank you." Ryan tapped the off button and quickly dressed.

There had been two names in the indictment against Randal for the illegal hunting—Red and June Hasting, his employees. They were first on his list to talk to this morning, after he broke the news to the widow. Lucky for him, the Hastings lived in a cabin on the Randal property.

First he'd head to Ruthie's and get a bite to eat. Walking into the diner, he was surprised to see so many locals. There was an empty stool beside Treat at the counter. Ryan sat and smiled at Ruthie who held up a coffee pot. He nodded.

"Mornin' Detective. Do you know who that body is I hauled off the mountain yesterday?" Treat asked, holding up his cup for a refill.

"I do, but I can't say anything until I've contacted the next of kin." Ryan had a hard time not spilling the name. Treat and Ruthie both knew just about everything about everyone who was local to Huckleberry. It would be nice to get their take on the Hastings and Vivian Randal.

"Then it is someone local." Ruthie shook her head. "I don't like it when the mountain takes a life, but when it's someone you know, makes you wonder how much in harmony we are with the mountain."

Ryan stared at the African American woman talking like a Native American. "I didn't realize you were so in tune with nature."

Treat slapped him on the back. "Ruthie lived with an old Indian woman after her father ran off and her mother sunk into depression."

Ruthie glared at Treat. "You may be my fiancé, but that doesn't give you the right to spill my business without asking." Ruthie pivoted and headed to the kitchen.

"Way to go, Treat. I didn't get to order anything." Ryan glared at the man but found Ruthie's upbringing interesting. No wonder Shandra frequented the café.

Treat looked like a whipped pup. "I didn't mean to make her uncomfortable, I was explaining how her moods ebb and flow with the seasons and nature."

"Don't worry, I'll not say anything. If I'm not getting any breakfast, I need to get going." Ryan downed his coffee and dropped a dollar on the counter.

"It's my fault. Take this." Treat slapped an egg from his plate between two pieces of toast.

"I'll just grab donuts on the way out of town."

"And be stereotyped. Here." Treat grabbed his hand and slapped the makeshift sandwich in Ryan's palm.

"Thanks. I think." Ryan left the restaurant, eating the sandwich as he walked to his Tahoe.

The Randal ranch was two miles beyond the turn off to Shandra's. He knew she'd be waiting to hear who the victim was, but his first priority was to inform the family.

He hated the job of telling family their loved one was gone. When it was murder it was even harder. Natural causes people could understand, but a violent death such as a car wreck or murder, that always left the family stunned.

Turning off the county road onto the Randal property was a night and day difference from Shandra's concealed, rough road. A large archway, with metal-art elk heads and the sign RANDAL RANCH signaled the wide, paved road that led into the forest.

The lane was nearly a mile long and lined with statuesque pine trees. The underbrush had been cleared back on both sides of the road a good twenty feet. At the end of the lane stood a large, pretentious, log home. Shandra's log home was small and tasteful. The Randal home looked like a lodge in a magazine. Next to it stood a four-door log garage. On either side of the garage stood huge cottonwood trees. Beyond the garage sat a small cabin and a barn.

Ryan stopped his SUV at the end of a river-rock

walkway that led up to the double, stained-glass doors. A few yellow leaves drifted by in the breeze as he walked up the cobbled path. A large knocker in the shape of an elk head hung on the wall on the left side of the doors. When he grasped the ring to knock, the sound of a bull elk bellowed through the house.

This guy had elk fever. Ryan waited for several minutes before he raised a hand to "bellow" again. The second elk call was answered by an exotic-looking woman of about forty. She wasn't Vivian Randal.

"I'm Detective Greer with the Weippe County Sheriff's Department." He pointed to the shield attached to his belt. "I'd like to speak with Mrs. Randal, please."

The color drained from the woman's face. "Is this about J.W.?"

"I'm not at liberty to say. Would you please get Mrs. Randal?" Ryan stepped into the house and closed the door.

The woman wrung her hands a second or two. "Sure. Yes, I'll get Mrs. Randal." Her own statement seemed to jostle her feet into motion.

Ryan stood by the door scanning the interior. The foyer was large and opened into a room as big as the whole Weippe County Sheriff's office. As he'd imagined, there were several bull elk heads mounted on the walls, as well as bear hides and a cougar body mount. The man had been a serious trophy collector.

He heard the click of heels on the hardwood flooring. Following the sound, he spied a tall, blonde woman walking toward him. His first impression was that of watching a model on a commercial. She carried herself tall, her shoulders drawn back, accentuating her full breasts that bounced with each step under a skin-tight pink shift. Her hair flowed free around her face and shoulders with just the right wave. Her long legs were clad in the same snug leggings Shandra had worn not that long ago. Her high-heeled boots stopped just below her knees.

"Oh! We have company!" The woman lengthened her stride and stopped in front of him. "We never get good-looking guys like you visiting. It's always stodgy old men."

The voice and seeing her up close, Ryan logged the young woman in at early twenties.

"I'm Detective Greer. I'm here to see Mrs. Randal." He extended his hand to shake. "Who are you?"

"I'm Cecily Wagner. Vivian is my aunt." She glanced over her shoulder. "Is that why June rushed by me? To get my aunt?"

"Yes."

"Well, she went outside, not into my aunt's study. Wait here, I'll get Aunt Vivian."

Chapter Seven

Shandra woke to Sheba barking. She found two trailer loads of horses, along with deputies and searchers, in her driveway. She dressed quickly and saddled up Apple to escort the group to the area where she'd found the body the previous day. Her dream had quelled any fears of the mountain.

"Where you headed?" Lil asked, walking into the barn with Lewis wrapped around her neck like an orange stole.

Shandra smiled. After two years living with the woman, she should be used to the cat and her purple combinations. Today, Lil had on a bright purple, thermal shirt under an open denim shirt with embroidered lavender flowers. Her pants were gray with purple and neon green flower patches on the knees.

"I'm going to escort the search crew to the site." She led Apple out of the barn and swung up on his back.

"You sure that's a good idea? Could be poachers that killed that man." Lil grabbed hold of Apple's reins.

"With all the cops around trying to discover how that poor man died, I'm sure any poachers are long gone." *Besides, I know I'm safe, Ella told me so.* Shandra smiled at her employee. "Please release the reins. I'll be fine."

Lil shook her head, but she released the reins. "You got your phone?"

"Yes."

"Call if you run into trouble."

"I will."

Shandra headed Apple up the trail with eight people following behind.

~*~

Yellow tape ringed the area where the body was found and streamers of yellow hung from trees in the direction she and Ryan had walked.

"Want me to help you search," she asked Deputy Trapp, who had spent the night on the mountain.

"We're good. You can go back home."

Ryan probably told him to keep her out of this. "Ok." Once she rode out of sight of the group, she cut back towards the fence neighboring the Randals. She'd do a quick fence line check from here down. If she found nothing, she'd steer clear of the search and check the fence above.

Apple picked his way through the underbrush until the fence stopped them. Shandra headed him downhill. Fifty feet down the fence line they ran into a well-used path that continued under the fence and onto the other property.

She dismounted and checked the fence. It was rigged to look untampered but was attached like a gate. She unhooked the wires, opened the gate, and led Apple through. Not knowing if the Randals had cattle on their property, she closed the fence.

Mounting, she headed Apple down the easy-to-follow trail. She was going to find out why this path had a convenient opening to her property.

~*~

Ryan watched the young woman stride down the same hall where the first woman had disappeared. Within seconds, she reappeared with the woman whose face he connected with Vivian Randal from his research on the internet.

"Aunt Vivian, this is Detective Greer." The young woman made the introduction with a hint of glee in her tone.

"Mrs. Randal, could we sit?" Ryan waved his hand toward the living area.

"Yes, of course. How long have you been waiting in my foyer?" Her clipped, well-spoken words seemed out of place with her surroundings.

"Not long." Ryan waited for the two women to sit on the couch. He took a seat on a chair near the couch. "When was the last time you saw your husband?"

"J.W.?" She tipped her head to the left. "Two days ago? He said he had a business meeting."

"Where was the meeting?" Ryan pulled out his notepad.

Her gaze latched onto the notepad. "Why are you asking me these questions?"

"Mrs. Randal, I'm afraid I have some bad news. Your husband's body—"

"Body? That means he's…" Her right hand clenched the arm of the couch. The niece slid closer.

"Yes. Your neighbor found J.W.'s body on her property yesterday." Ryan wasn't going to state his condition.

"Why didn't you contact me yesterday?" She leaned forward. "Why wait this long?"

"It took us a while to determine who he was. He didn't have any identification on him."

"But surely someone would have recognized him." Instead of falling apart the woman was using anger.

"He'd been in the woods long enough the animals…"

Mrs. Randal closed her eyes and swallowed twice, loudly.

"I'm sorry to have to give you the news. During the autopsy, death by natural causes was ruled out." Ryan held his gaze on the two women, watching for anything that might lead him to believe one of them put the bullet through the man's heart.

"What does that mean?" Cecily asked.

"He was killed by a bullet to the heart."

Mrs. Randal's eyes widened for a moment, then shuttered away any thoughts she might be having.

The younger woman gasped and raised a hand to her mouth.

"Why would anyone put a bullet in Uncle John's heart?" Cecily asked, peering at her aunt.

Mrs. Randal shook her head and patted her niece's hand.

"Mrs. Randal, why would your husband be in the woods if he told you he was on a business trip?" Ryan wondered why the woman thought her husband was gone when he was only a couple miles away.

The elk bugling sound vibrated through the house.

"Who could that be? I don't want to see anyone, Cecily. Tell them to go away." Mrs. Randal waved her niece to answer the door.

~*~

Shandra stood in front of two massive doors hosting twin stained-glass windows. The image on the glass appeared to be elk, a bull and a cow. When the door knocker sounded like an elk bugle, she confirmed her original assumption about J.W. Randal.

A door opened. A young, gorgeous blonde with tear-filled eyes stood in the slight opening.

"We aren't taking visitors right now." She moved to shut the door.

Shandra shoved her body into the opening. "I'm not leaving here until I find out why someone has a path from this house through a hidden gate and onto my property."

The young woman tried to block her path, but Shandra was quicker. "I'd like to speak with Mr. or Mrs. Randal." Her steps faltered when she spotted Ryan sitting in a chair and Mrs. Randal facing him from a couch.

Ryan stood. "What are you doing here?"

"I led the searchers to the site then followed my fence line and found a well-worn path from my property, through a hidden gate, and straight to the barn behind this house." She glanced at Mrs. Randal and back at Ryan. From the somber atmosphere and the tears pooling in the women's eyes, she'd bet her next vase the body she'd found was J.W.'s.

Chapter Eight

If the body was J.W. and he was found on the mountain, chances were the women didn't have a clue about the path. Shandra tamped down the anger she'd fed as she and Apple followed the trail.

"Mrs. Randal, I'm sorry for your loss." She walked sedately down and stood next to Ryan. The tendon on the side of his jaw twitched. He wasn't as happy to see her as she was to see him. It stung a bit. But she also understood he'd told her to not investigate on her own and here she was, popping into his questioning.

"Mrs. Randal, Miss Higheagle is the person who found your husband's body." Ryan's tone reflected his annoyance at her "dropping by".

Vivian glared up at Shandra. "What was he doing on your land?" she accused.

"That's what I'd like to know. Especially after finding that hidden gate and path." Shandra could tell by the glint in the woman's eye, she had the notion J.W.

and Shandra were seeing one another. Which would lead to a lot of suspects if he had a roving eye.

"Evidence shows he was killed on your property and animals dragged his body onto Miss Higheagle's side of the fence." Ryan motioned for Shandra to sit.

She took the chair farthest away from the group. The young woman sat on the couch next to Vivian.

"Mrs. Randal, your answers will help us find the person who killed your husband." Ryan poised his pen over his notepad.

A shiver slithered up Shandra's backbone. So it was murder.

"He told me Sunday evening that he would be out of town at a business meeting." Vivian stole a quick glance at the young woman.

"Did he say where the meeting would be?" Ryan's gaze was locked on the woman.

"No. He never told me about his meetings. He said the only business I needed to tend to was my own and to be a gracious hostess when he had big game hunters here on the weekends."

Shandra latched onto the contempt in her voice. This was an unhappy woman. Was she unhappy enough to want to be a widow rather than a divorcee?

"What vehicle did he take for his business meeting?" Ryan continued with questions.

Vivian stared at the young woman. "I haven't been out of the house. Cecily, when you went to the resort yesterday, what vehicle was missing?"

Cecily shook her head, making her long, blonde waves shudder. "All the cars were there. The Humvee, Jeep, BMW convertible, and my car."

"Where would your husband have been if he didn't

leave in a vehicle?" Ryan tapped the point of his pen on the notepad as he watched the two women.

Shandra squirmed. She had questions of her own, but knew to open her mouth would only put more points against her.

"Why did the lady who answered the door run out of here after letting me in?" Ryan asked.

Vivian perked up. "June let you in?" Her face slowly darkened with anger. "That slut! I thought she'd been sleeping with J.W." Vivian stood and paced the floor. "Cecily, call over to the cabin and tell June and Red to get over here."

"Don't tell them why, just ask them to come over," Ryan added.

Cecily left the room. Shandra suspected it was to make the call on an intercom between the two residences. Her step-father had such a thing between his office and the foreman's shack.

Ryan couldn't believe his good luck. Soon he'd have all the main suspects in this case in the same room. He glanced at Shandra. If she kept still, he might have a chance at cracking this case before his brother's wedding. He'd hate to have to cancel when everyone, including himself, was anxious for him to escort Shandra to the wedding.

Cecily returned. "I told Red you requested to see him and June." She sat back down by her aunt.

"Do you need to show them in?" Shandra asked.

Ryan shook his head imperceptibly at the interfering woman.

"No, they'll come through the back door." Cecily didn't act as if her aunt's outburst had been out of character, which didn't fit the description Hazel gave him of Mrs. Randal. Perhaps she was one person in public and another in private.

"Mrs. Randal!" a male voice called from the back of the house.

"In the great room, Red," Vivian called back.

Ryan turned his attention to the couple walking down the hall. The man, Red, was tall, trim, and muscular. He sported a red beard and close-cropped red hair. He wore the usual clothes of an outdoorsman. Jeans, flannel shirt, and cowboy boots. June wore a loose sweater over a blue T-shirt, jeans, and leather loafers. Her dark hair and exotic dark eyes were the opposite of Mrs. Randal's polished make-up and bottle-blonde hair.

"You wanted to speak to us?" Red asked, moving his wife into the room with a hand on her back.

June's eyes were red and swollen.

"Actually, I would like to speak with you." Ryan stood. "I'm Detective Greer of the Weippe County Sheriff's Department."

Red looked down at his wife. "This have anything to do with J.W. being missing?"

Ryan watched the couple. They had something they were keeping between them. "Yes. It does. Miss Higheagle found his body on her property yesterday."

June turned into her husband's chest and wept.

"You'll have to excuse my wife, she's real emotional these days." Red wrapped his arms around June and stared back at Ryan.

"Why would Mr. Randal tell his wife he was going away on business, not take a vehicle, and end up dead on his own property?" Ryan hoped Shandra was watching Vivian and Cecily because he was facing the Hastings.

"Could be because he wanted to shoot a big bull he knew was on the property. Since he was hauled in for the illegal tags, he's been obsessed with killing a six point he spotted while taking Mr. Takagi on a hunt." Red's voice held as much contempt as Vivian's had.

"I told him if he set foot on the mountain to kill another animal while all the investigating and trials were going on, I'd turn him in myself," Vivian added.

"He faked his trip just to go after an elk?" Shandra's disbelief rang in her voice.

"He had the fever bad," Red added.

"But an elk doesn't shoot back." Ryan shifted so he could keep an eye on all four of the suspects.

"What do you mean?" Red asked, tightening his hold on his wife.

"J.W. died from a bullet in the heart."

"No!" wailed June. She pushed out of her husband's arms and stared up into his face. "Why?"

Ryan found the result he was searching for.

"You think I did it?" Red stared at his wife, his mouth open, his eyes beseeching.

"You turned him in for the illegal hunts." Her sobs muffled her words.

Ryan understood enough to realize Red knew about his wife and his boss. "Red, were you with J.W. when he went on his last hunt?"

"No. Until this morning, I've spent all week in this house repairing a water leak in the washroom." He swept his arm toward Vivian and Cecily. "They know, they were complaining about the noise."

"That's true, detective. Red finished the job last night." Vivian smiled at Red. "And he did a wonderful job."

By the blush on the man's cheeks, he either had a crush on the woman or the two were playing footsie just like his wife and her husband.

Ryan's phone vibrated. He glanced at the number. Rickman. "I have to take this." He walked out into the foyer and slid his finger across the screen.

"What else do you have for me?"

Chapter Nine

Shandra silently thanked whoever was calling Ryan and turned to Red. "I'm Shandra Higheagle. I own the property on the west side of here."

Red's gaze bounced off her to the mantle behind.

"This morning after taking the search party to the murder site, I decided to ride my fence line. I found a well-used trail from my property to the back of the barn here. At the fence, I discovered a cleverly hidden gate. Do you have any idea why someone from here would be coming onto my property?"

Red cleared his throat but didn't utter a word.

"Red, what other illegal things had J.W. been doing? It seems I didn't know the man I married at all," Vivian said, standing and pacing between the couch and the large, river-rock fireplace.

"Viv—Mrs. Randal, I hate to say this but I don't think a penny of the money your husband has made was legally." Red's face turned a crimson with this statement.

"What was he doing illegally on my property?" Shandra's ire was up. The man was trespassing *and* he was doing something illegal.

"He had that fake gate put in, so when a paying hunter was here and the elk were on your property or farther north, I could round them up and drive them back over here." Red shook his head. "He knew it would be suspicious to put up a high fence to keep the animals in. He had wildlife cameras set up in all the places the elk liked to hang out, so we knew where they were most of the time."

"Are some of those cameras on my property?" Talk about invasion of privacy.

"Yes, Ma'am. There are two up on the highest areas of your property. There's a big herd likes to hang out on the edge of your property and the National Forest above you."

Knowing those cameras were on her property gave her a sense of vulnerability and creepiness. She faced Vivian. "I want any cameras your husband put up on my property removed today."

Vivian spoke to Red. "I want all cameras you installed for J.W. removed from Shandra's and our property. There will be no more illegal anything going on here."

Ryan returned to the room. "Did I hear something about cameras? Where?"

"Apparently all over Huckleberry Mountain," Shandra said, glaring at Red. She knew the man was only following orders, but still.

"Mr. Hastings what can you tell me about the cameras?" Ryan had his notepad out and pen perched above it.

"J.W. had me place wildlife cameras in the areas the elk frequented most."

"Two are on my property." Shandra still couldn't believe the gall of her neighbor. "How long have they been up?"

"About four years. We switched in new ones last year." Red was becoming less embarrassed as they talked about the cameras.

"How many are on this property?" Ryan asked. "And where?"

"We set-up eight on J.W.'s property. They're at every spot the elk cross the fences and one where they tend to bed down."

"How do you monitor their activity? Do you have to pick up the SD cards every day?" Ryan stared at the other man.

Shandra could tell by the blankness on Ryan's face he was asking an important question. A flash like lightning sparked in her head. If there was a camera near the murder site they'd get a look at the killer.

Movement by the hallway caught her attention. Mrs. Hastings was headed down the hall. It wasn't her place to call the woman back. Shandra moved closer to Ryan. He glanced at her and she nodded to the hall.

"Mrs. Hastings, please remain with everyone else." Ryan's voice carried down the hall with authority.

The woman jumped, pivoted, and scurried back to stand just behind her husband.

"Mrs. Hastings, where were you going?" Ryan asked.

Shandra watched the other woman. She was more

shook up about J.W.'s death than the wife. There was no way the husband couldn't see it. She studied Red. He didn't appear to be upset by his wife's crying over their boss. But he had said he'd turned his boss in for the illegal hunting. Was that his way of getting back at the man who was sleeping with his wife?

"I wanted to check on some things I had started in the kitchen." She wiped her runny nose with the sleeve of her sweater.

Vivian made a sound akin to disgust.

The two women were from completely different worlds. It was easy to see why J.W. married Vivian. The woman was the epitome of class and style. June reminded her of a favorite stuffed animal, snuggly and needing nurtured. Was that the appeal she had to both her husband and her boss?

"I'm sure it's nothing that will burn," Vivian said, pacing once again. "Do you have any idea what he was doing on the mountain? And where did he stay if his car was in the garage?"

June visibly shrank against her husband.

Shandra had a pretty good idea where the man has been. She wasn't going to say anything to the group, but she'd voice her opinion to Ryan when they were alone.

Ryan scanned the people in the room. The wife wasn't as distraught as he'd expected. Her niece seemed to be there for Vivian. Knowing that, he decided to continue the interrogation with everyone present.

"I've come to the assumption your husband was after that six-point Mr. Hastings said he'd been eyeing. From what we've discovered, the body was shot on this property next to a large bull elk missing his antlers." Ryan studied Red. "It's my belief whoever killed Mr. Randal has those antlers."

"There's only one other person who knew about that six-point. Mr. Takagi," Red said.

"My uncle was talking on the phone to Mr. Takagi on Sunday," Cecily added. "It sounded like they were going to meet somewhere."

Ryan jotted down the name. "Any idea how I can contact him?"

Vivian stood. "J.W. kept a list of his shooting buddies in his office. I'll get you the phone number."

"Thank you." Ryan turned his attention to Red. "Mr. Hasting, what can you tell me about the wildlife cameras? How do you access the information on them?"

"The cameras that are within two miles of the barn are set up on monitors, the others I have to gather the SD cards once a week, usually on Friday before hunters were coming in. That way J.W. knew where to take the hunters."

"When Mrs. Randal returns with the phone number, I want to see the monitors." Ryan closed his notepad and motioned to Shandra. He led the woman to the foyer.

"I want you to go back home. I'll come by tonight and we can compare notes." He leaned close and talked low. He didn't want the others to know he bounced theories off the woman. And it gave him a chance to inhale her unique scent of earth, horse, and herbs.

"I want to find the cameras on my property and destroy them."

The artist liked her privacy. Why else would she live at the end of a barely navigable road on the side of a mountain?

"I'll see that all the cameras are taken down. I'm hoping one will have our killer."

Her eyes lit up. "I knew that's what you were thinking."

Vivian's heels clicked as she walked toward them. "Here is George Takagi's number." She stopped within arm's length of him and Shandra. Dropping her voice she added. "I'd take a look at June. I think she'd been pressuring him to leave me."

Ryan had thought as much.

Shandra's eyebrows raised.

"Yes, I know the two have been fooling around. He couldn't keep his hands off any female he knew was off limits. I caught him making passes at Cecily a month ago. I threatened to walk out on him and not help with his legal fees if he touched her again." Vivian's cheeks reddened. "I don't want to sound like I killed him, but quite frankly, whoever killed him did me a favor." She spun on her heel and rejoined her niece on the couch.

"Wow! Do you think she said that to throw suspicion off her?" Shandra whispered.

"We'll soon see." Ryan grasped the door knob and opened the door. "Go home."

Shandra lingered beside him a moment as if undecided. Her face brightened. A wisp of a smile tipped her lips and she exited the house.

He didn't know what she was up to, but he was pretty sure she wouldn't just go home and leave solving the case to him.

Chapter Ten

Shandra mounted Apple and turned him back up the path she'd followed to the Randal barn. Was there a camera in the area they believed J.W. was shot? If so, had the search crew found it? Getting caught nosing around there would only make Ryan keep her in the dark. She'd check around the area of the hidden gate, though that wasn't a spot she'd think elk would cross. But there had to be several spots above the murder site where they crossed her fence. Red said there were two cameras on her property.

Tomorrow, she'd take Lil with her and see if they could find the cameras. It was too late today to ride back to get Lil, ride the length of the fence line, and get back home before dark. With autumn coming the days grew shorter.

At the hidden gate, she snooped around the bushes and trees looking for a camera on both sides of the fence. Nothing. She climbed back up on Apple and made a straight line toward home. No sense in asking how the search was going, they wouldn't tell her anything.

Sheba greeted her when she rode out of the trees.

"Hi girl!" Shandra dismounted and ruffled the dog's ears. Sheba had been getting her morning snack from Lil when Shandra left. She hadn't called the dog to go along.

"Where you been all morning? Doesn't take that long to ride them searchers in and back." Lil said, walking into the barn.

"I decided to ride the fence line down to the county road and discovered a gate and trail that took me to the Randal barn. Ryan was there. The body is J.W.'s." She placed the saddle on the rack. "And he was killed."

Lil nodded her head. "I believe that. He's been a thorn in lots of people's sides for a long time."

"What really irks is he had wildlife cameras set up on my property. Red Hastings, his employee, told me. That's why they put in the gate, to access the cameras and chase the elk to them." Saying it again started her blood boiling. The nerve of the man!

"I believe he'd chase the animals over to shoot, and really, if a man stoops that low, I can believe the cameras as well." Lil scooped grain and poured it in a bucket on the wall in front of Apple.

"It also seems J.W. liked the ladies. You heard any rumors about him fooling around?" Shandra planned to have a late lunch in town and see if she could find some gossip at Ruthie's.

"Not so much rumors as seen him locking lips with a girl that looked too young." Lil untied Apple and led him to the corral.

Vivian said he'd made moves on her niece. What other young girl had he been seeing?

"I'm heading to town. Do you need anything?" Shandra waited a beat. Lil didn't reply, meaning she needed nothing. "Come on Sheba." She hurried into the house, cleaned up, and she and Sheba hopped into the Jeep.

~*~

Ryan sat in a small room in the Randal barn studying the four monitors. "How come there isn't a signal coming from this camera?" He pointed to the upper right monitor.

"Something could have happened to the camera."

Red had been reluctant to allow Ryan into the room without a search warrant, but Mrs. Randal had ordered the man to allow Ryan access to anything he wanted.

"Do you have a map that shows where this camera is located?" Ryan's gut said it would be near where the man was shot.

Red rummaged in a drawer and pulled out a geographic map. "Here." He placed his finger in an area close to Shandra's property line.

"That's the area where Mr. Randal was shot." Ryan watched the other man closely. He didn't even twitch. Either he had more nerves than he'd displayed so far or the spot meant nothing to him.

Ryan pulled out a radio. With cell phones getting scanty reception on this side of the mountain, he'd brought the radio along to keep in contact with the searchers.

"Deputy Speaks, can you hear me, this is Detective Greer. Over."

The radio crackled.

"Deputy Speaks, this is Detective Greer. Over."

"This is Speaks. Over."

"Have you found any wildlife cameras or surveillance cameras? Over."

"Negative. Over."

Ryan looked at Hastings. "How far from the fence line was it?"

"About twenty feet off the fence line. It was on the base of a fir tree."

"Speaks, check a fir tree about twenty feet from the fence line. If the camera's gone, the person who killed him knew it was there. Over." He stared at Hastings. "Who besides you and Randal knew about the cameras?"

Hastings ran a hand over his face. "June, Mrs. Randal. I think Cecily knew about them but she wouldn't know where they were. She isn't the outdoor type."

"No one else? What about hunters. Did Randal show them the cameras?" If the man said no, then the pool of suspects was small.

"Only two. Takagi who was fined and wasn't happy when he found out about the illegal tags, and Todd Smith. But he's the one who helped J.W. research and pick out the cameras."

"Smith and Randal were friends?" Ryan jotted the name down on his notepad.

"Yeah, they go back clear to high school, I believe." Red's feet shuffled back and forth. "I don't like leaving June alone."

Ryan studied the man. "You knew your wife was sleeping with your employer."

Hastings bit his lip and tears glistened in his eyes. "He gave her things I couldn't. He wooed her with money and then the ability to give her a child." He wiped a flannel sleeve under his nose. "She's pregnant with his child, but I plan to help her raise it as if it's ours." He raised his chin. "Don't tell Mrs. Randal. I don't want her knowing."

"You must love your wife very much to raise another man's child. A child that was conceived through adultery." Ryan wanted to see if the man would snap. If perhaps he had snapped and killed J.W. Randal in a fit of rage.

"I do love my wife. She's wanted a child for years, but I couldn't make it happen."

"With Randal out of the way, you don't have to worry about him coming along and taking your wife and child." Rubbing salt into wounds wasn't pleasant, but he had to see how much the man could take and not break.

"I didn't want to kill him. I turned him in to Fish and Game. I wanted him to be financially unable to try and take June or the baby if he decided he wanted an heir." Red waved a hand in front of the monitors. "You through in here?"

"I'll have a deputy come over and go with you to collect all the cameras and these monitors." Ryan stood, slid his notepad in his pocket, and walked out of the room.

Red closed the door and locked it.

The radio crackled. Ryan strode toward his vehicle before answering. "Greer. Over."

"We found some wire around a tree but no camera.

Over."

"Bag it. I'm headed to town to start interviewing suspects. Send a deputy to the Randal house to collect the monitors and ride the mountain with Red Hasting to pick up the wildlife cameras scattered around. Over."

"We're about through here. I'll send Trapp. The rest of us should be in town about dark. Over."

Ryan climbed in his SUV and headed down the lane and out to the county road. He had a hard time passing Shandra's driveway, but he needed to contact George Takagi, Fish and Game, and Todd Smith. He had to rule them out before he zeroed in on the family and employees of the murdered man.

Chapter Eleven

Shandra sat at the counter in Ruthie's Café sipping on her caramel shake, waiting for her cheeseburger and sweet potato fries.

"What can you tell me about Vivian Randal?" Shandra asked Ruthie. It was mid-afternoon, and she was the only customer.

"That woman has her manicured fingers in every charity in this town." Ruthie said through the window between the counter area and the kitchen.

"What's your impression of her? You know, bossy, soft-spoken, egotistical?"

Ruthie laughed. "Why do you want to know my opinion of the woman?"

"Well, it doesn't have to be your opinion. What have you heard others say about her?" Shandra wanted to learn more about the woman who, in her opinion, was cold enough to kill her husband.

"She doesn't come in here much. I don't think

she's the burger and shake type." Ruthie placed Shandra's meal in front of her, filled a glass with ice and water, and came around the counter to sit on the stool next to Shandra.

She swallowed half the water and set it down. Ruthie ran her fingers up and down the glass chasing the condensation. "June Hasting, who works for the Randals, comes in quite a bit. What I've heard from her is J.W. wasn't nice to his wife, but he treated his help well. She said Mrs. Randal was confrontational and expected one woman to do the work of three."

"What about the niece? Cicely, I think." Shandra picked at her fries.

"She's in here a lot. Usually with a different guy. I haven't heard her say much about her aunt and uncle." Ruthie took another swallow, set the glass down, and faced Shandra. "Why so many questions about the Randals?"

"It was J.W.'s body I found yesterday." Shandra figured if Ruthie didn't already know she would soon enough.

"I heard it was some hiker tangled with the wildlife." Ruthie took another sip.

"Someone shot him and left him for the animals." Shandra shivered. It was one cold-blooded human that murdered another.

"You think it was his wife?" Ruthie's eyes widened.

"I don't know. I was over there this morning when Ryan interviewed them. She didn't seem too shook up about the whole thing." But if he treated her poorly, perhaps his death was a relief.

Ruthie shook her head. "I can't see Vivian Randal

picking up a gun, let alone shooting someone."

"You never know what some people are capable of." Shandra thought of the professor in college she'd fallen in love with only to find out the hard way he hid a side no one knew about.

"Can you think of anyone who would like to shoot J.W.?" Shandra took a bite of her burger. Ruthie made the best cheeseburgers.

"There is probably a whole line. I'd think the first person on the list would be the Takagi fella who got caught in the illegal hunting-tag mess."

The door jingled as an older couple wandered into the café.

Ruthie smiled. "Afternoon, Mr. and Mrs. Cyrus." She picked up menus and sauntered over to the booth where the couple sat.

Shandra continued eating and puzzling things in her head. She'd noticed two pieces of art in the Randal home by an artist that her friends, Ted and Naomi Norton, supported in their gallery, Dimensions. That would be her next stop to learn more about the Randals.

~*~

Ryan drove down the main street of Huckleberry and spotted Shandra walking into Dimensions Gallery. He smiled remembering how tenacious she'd been protecting her friend Naomi Norton when she was the prime suspect in the murder where he and Shandra met.

He crept by the gallery, peering in the windows. The two women were hugging. Picking up speed, he headed the vehicle on through town and out to the Fish and Game building on the road toward the resort. Seemed odd to have the building close to the ski resort and not on the side of town that boasted the most National Forest land, but then this was the government they were talking about.

At the Fish and Game office, people moved about inside like an overstaffed restaurant. One young woman sat behind a desk at the front of all the activity.

"I'm Detective Greer with the Weippe County Sheriff's Department. I'd like to speak with the person in charge of game violations, please." Ryan smiled at the woman.

"That would be Tate Pearce." She picked up a phone, tapped three numbers and waited.

"Mr. Pearce, there's a Sheriff's office Detective here to see you." She nodded and replaced the phone. "He'll be right out."

Ryan scanned the beehive mentality of the building and asked, "Is it always this busy in here?"

The young woman nodded. "You'd think they could sit down and get more work done wouldn't you?"

A man in his mid-thirties emerged from a door at the back of the building. He strode forward and extended his hand. "Tate Pearce. How can I help you?" He directed Ryan to walk outside with him.

"Mr. Pearce, I'd like to know the allegations and actions being taken against J.W. Randal and any accomplices." Ryan fished his notepad out of his pocket and poised his pen ready to write.

Pearce whistled. "That's an ongoing investigation. After the initial call and one of our officers investigated, we discovered multiple infractions."

"Who was the officer?" Ryan asked.

"Melvin Clower. He's our best field officer."

"I'd like to visit with him about J.W. Randal."

Ryan studied the man.

Pearce shook his head. "The case is confidential until it is all settled in court."

"J.W. Randal was found dead in the forest. He'd been shot. I need to talk to Clower to see if one of the other people named in the investigation may have decided to take revenge on Randal."

Pearce took a step back. "J.W. was killed? I heard there was a body brought out, but I figured it was a hiker. Man." He spun toward the building. "I'll get Melvin's number for you. Damn. I wanted this investigation to go to court to scare other illegal hunters."

Ryan followed the man into the building. Maybe if the poachers knew Randal was shot in the heart, they'd be less likely to take illegal game.

~*~

Shandra sat in the backroom of Dimensions Gallery visiting with her friends, Ted and Naomi. This was their first visit since Shandra's return from the art show in New Mexico.

"How was the show? Did you pick up any more clients?" Ted asked, always thinking ahead to potential buyers.

"I sold one vase and handed out your cards to a couple-dozen people who were interested but wanted to talk it over either with significant others or business partners." Shandra sipped the tea Naomi set to brewing after their initial hello.

"How did the classes you taught go?" Naomi asked. This was why the couple made great gallery owners. Naomi cared about the art and how each piece came to be, and Ted watched the numbers.

"I had enthusiastic students in both classes, but the all-day workshop at the reservation was by far the best part of the trip." She'd contacted the school at the Apache Jicarillo Reservation about working with the children and how they can put emotion into clay.

"I bet you were a hit. You have a way with people." Naomi patted her arm.

Shandra leaned back in her chair. "I noticed two pieces by Lionel over at the Randal house today. I know Mrs. Randal purchased one of my vases last year at the June event, what other art work does she like?"

Naomi raised an eyebrow. "What were you doing at Vivian Randal's house?"

Leave it to her friend to pick up on that instead of answer the question, which she really didn't want the answer to, but found it a good way to move into what she really wanted to ask.

"I discovered her husband's body yesterday."

"No! Not another body. Shandra you have to stop finding bodies, it will get back to your clients and they may—"

"Love it!" Ted looked up from the computer. "If you keep finding bodies, we can use that in promotion." He moved his hand in the air as if reading a billboard. "Potter not only digs up clay but bodies."

Shandra laughed. "No, thank you. I'd rather not have my art bought because I'm all of a sudden stumbling over bodies."

"So why did you really bring up the art work at the Randals?" Naomi, straight to the point.

"I wanted your thoughts on the couple and each as an individual." Shandra took a sip of tea.

"You think Vivian killed J.W.?" Naomi slid her chair closer, like two school girls gossiping.

"I don't know. I just want to know more about them and the niece that lives with them." She paused and smiled. "And their employees, June and Red Hasting."

"I don't know the Hastings other than seeing them in Ruthie's now and then. I've not visited with the wife." Naomi sipped her tea and continued. "The niece has come in here a couple times with Vivian. She was polite, gave her aunt her studied opinion on art pieces, and seemed nice." She smiled. "Vivian…I've talked with her in public and private. She's a woman who is better one on one than in a crowd. In a group setting she tends to shrink to the back."

"I don't understand. How can she be so busy and influential with all her charities if she shrinks to the background in group settings?" Shandra was having a hard time understanding the woman.

"She takes the other members to lunch, and gets someone who is good with crowds to do the mingling. But her name is listed on everything because she is good at opening pockets and check books." Naomi frowned. "I have seen on a couple of occasions where J.W. treated her like a servant girl. His comments were nasty and cutting." She tapped a finger against the teacup. "If I were Vivian, I'd have found a way to get rid of him long ago."

Shandra stared at her friend. While she knew, and had impressed upon Ryan, that Naomi wasn't a killer, she saw there was a point in which Naomi would sever her relationship if it became unbearable.

She looked deep inside herself. A person could also revert to the fight-or-flight instinct if pushed too far. She had. Repressing memories of her last night with Carl Landers, she pulled her thoughts back to the present.

"But the key is: do you think Vivian capable of murder?" Shandra asked.

"How was he killed?" Ted asked.

"A shot to the heart."

"Ouch." Ted rubbed his chest.

"That sounds like a crime of passion." Naomi shook her head. "I can't see Vivian using a gun. I could see her poisoning J.W., but not a gun."

Shandra had the same thought while sitting in the Randal home. While the decorating was that of a hunting lodge, she could tell the woman wasn't comfortable in the setting. "I wonder how long before all the hunting-lodge décor disappears from that house," she mused out loud.

Chapter Twelve

Ryan had located George Takagi. He was willing to have a conference call with his lawyer present from his office in Seattle, Washington.

Chief Sandberg had given Ryan permission to use his office and phone to do the interview.

"Want me to make you a pot of coffee in case this goes long?" the chief asked.

"No, I'm fine." If he had to drink the battery acid the chief called coffee, he'd never make it through the interview.

"Ok, I'll go do some PR work." The chief donned a ball cap with the initials HPD and slipped into a military looking jacket.

"Where do you go to do Public Relations work?" Ryan couldn't imagine in a community this size that the man had to do anything to get re-elected.

"Ruthie's and Daily Donut." The man grinned and headed out the door.

"Have fun." Ryan sat down behind the desk. He picked up the phone and dialed the number written in his notepad.

"Takagi and Sons. How may I direct your call?" answered a mature female voice.

"George Takagi, please." Ryan waited while elevator-type music floated out of the phone receiver.

"Takagi." The strong, confident voice that answered didn't surprise Ryan.

"Mr. Takagi, this is Detective Greer. Is your lawyer there so we can do the interview?"

"One minute. I'll dial him in."

Silence and a click.

"Detective Greer, I have Clint Deaver, my attorney on the other line," Takagi said.

"Mr. Deaver, I'm questioning your client about his interactions with J.W. Randal." A deep inhale on the other end made Ryan hastily add, "I'm not gathering any information for the illegal tag allegations."

"Why are you interested in my client's interactions with Randal?" The voice was not as deep as Takagi but sounded near the same age with a bit of a smoker's rasp.

"J.W. Randal was found on the property adjoining his two days ago. He'd been mauled by animals." Ryan wasn't going to give away everything. He heard an intake of air and a slight chuckle. He'd bet the chuckle was from Takagi.

"Good heavens! What does this have to do with my client?" The attorney must have been the one who'd gasped.

"I need Mr. Takagi to tell me the last time he saw the deceased and under what circumstances." Ryan tapped his pen on his notepad. Doing an interview like this over the phone only gave him half the answers. Watching the interviewees as they are being questioned filled in blanks and gave openings for deeper questions. "Keep in mind we know you called Sunday night and asked Randal to meet you."

"You don't have to answer these questions, George," Deaver suggested.

"I didn't meet with J.W. And I didn't call him, he called me. At the advice of Deaver, I was staying away from the man. It wasn't until I went hunting with J.W. that I discovered how reprehensible he was. When we'd met before I thought he was too cocky and full of himself, but when he gave his word I could bag a large bull elk on his property and the cost was cheaper than going to Montana, I thought, why not?" The sound of swallowing and thunk of a coffee cup being set down echoed in the phone.

"What did you discover while hunting with him?" Ryan was getting a pretty good picture of the deceased. From what he'd learned so far it was a miracle the man had lived as long as he had.

"He had no regard for any form of life. Once I'd bagged the bull, he shot every living thing we came across. It was ridiculous how trigger happy he was. And the way he treated his wife…she's probably glad he's dead."

"Did he physically abuse her in front of you?" Ryan reran his encounter with Mrs. Randal and hadn't noticed any bruising.

"Not physically. He called her names and belittled her at the one meal we all shared. It was as if he thought it made him look like more of a man. He was definitely overcompensating for something. Then to find out the tag he gave me wasn't in my name but that of his niece…getting eaten by the animals seems like justice."

"Did Mrs. Randal do or say anything to stand up for herself?" He couldn't believe the woman he'd met would sit there and take the verbal abuse.

"She smiled and said nothing." Takagi paused. "His death wasn't an accident. That's why you're asking all these questions."

"He was shot before the animals made a meal of him." Ryan had already determined Takagi wasn't the one to kill Randal. He was following his attorney's orders.

"Shot. You might want to look into their hired help. Red glared at Randal when he wasn't looking. Another suspect might be the niece. I looked out my bedroom window before going to bed and Randal had his hands all over her out back of the house. It didn't look like she was enjoying it." The disgust in Takagi's voice mirrored Ryan's thoughts.

He'd felt Red's animosity and figured Randal was fooling around with other women. But the niece? He hadn't seen that. I'll go back and interview the niece alone and see if the incident was before or after Mrs. Randal threatened her husband. "Thank you for your time."

"You're welcome. I hope his killer doesn't turn out to be Vivian."

The phone clicked twice, and Ryan hung up the receiver.

~*~

Shandra stepped out of Dimensions and spotted

Cicely entering the beauty shop down the street. She didn't normally stalk people, but her curiosity got the better of her and her hair could use the split ends trimmed.

With a determined stride, she hurried to the beauty shop and stepped inside to the jingling of tiny bells.

"Be with you in a minute!" called out a female voice from behind a partition.

Shandra usually trimmed her ends herself. This was her first time inside the tiny shop. The colors pink, white, and black exploded from every nook and cranny in the place. Even most of the product bottles on the floor to ceiling shelves to her left were black, white, or pink. The smell of chemicals and a sweet perfume hung heavy in the air.

A short, plump, young woman with spiked, pink hair emerged from behind the partition. "Hello. Welcome to Peggy's Hair Salon. I'm Tammy. How may we help you today?"

"Tammy, I just need to get my ends trimmed. Do you have an opening?" Shandra held back from trying to peek around the partition.

"I can do that. Follow me."

Shandra followed the woman around the partition and was rewarded with a seat right next to Cecily.

The young woman stopped mid-sentence and stared at her. "Are you following me?" she asked, scrunching her brows.

"No. I had getting my hair trimmed on my list of things to do today." She hated lying, but sometimes a little fib was better than saying, yes, I saw you come in here and wanted to see what you were like away from your aunt.

Tammy floated the big cape over Shandra's body.

"I've seen you somewhere before," Tammy said, spritzing the ends of Shandra's hair.

"You may have seen my photo in the paper. I'm Shandra Higheagle. I live on the old Whitmire place."

"Yeah! And you dug up a body there a couple months ago. Turned out to be Crazy Lil's long lost boyfriend." Tammy smiled and picked up a pair of scissors.

"She is also the person who found my uncle's body," Cecily added.

The tall, thin lady dressed all in black, with long black hair and one wide band of pink hair stopped her scissors and stared at Cecily in the mirror. "I'm sorry to hear that. Did he die of a heart attack?"

"No. Someone shot him," Cecily said matter-of-factly. She peered straight at Shandra in the mirror. "She and a detective think it was my aunt."

"No, Detective Greer and I don't think it was your aunt. He is talking to everyone who knew your uncle and may have had a grudge." Shandra didn't want to get linked with digging for clues, even though she was.

"A grudge?" The tall stylist questioned. "June Hasting was in here the other day. She wasn't happy with Mrs. Randal. She went on and on about how Mrs. Randal expected one person to do the work of three and then she started crying. Right here in my chair."

"That's ridiculous. She hasn't been given any extra chores. In fact, my uncle told my aunt to find another person to help June." Cecily pointed to her hair. "Take a little more off that side."

"Why would your uncle care if June's load was

lightened?" Shandra asked.

"I don't know. Maybe because he was sleeping with her. He was an asshole most of the time but every once in a while he'd do something that made you think he might be human after all." Cecily peered at her reflection in the mirror.

"You didn't care for your uncle?" Witnessing her lack of emotion earlier in the day, Shandra had took it for shock. Now she saw it was the fact Cecily hadn't cared for her uncle.

"He treated my aunt despicably, did illegal things, and he put his hands down every female's pants he could." The disgust oozed off her words.

"Did your aunt know about the women?" Shandra was finding more evidence against Vivian. Her gut didn't like it, but her mind could see how a woman could snap when she'd had enough.

"She knew and as long as he didn't come to her for what he was getting elsewhere she was content."

The stylist picked up a blow dryer and flipped the switch. There wasn't a chance to talk any more until she finished styling Cecily's hair.

Shandra glanced at her image in the mirror. "That's good! Don't take off any more." She'd been so caught up in her conversation she'd forgotten Tammy, who, was a little too scissor happy. Her hair was now three inches shorter than when she walked in.

"Thank you. How much do I owe you?" She stood, removing the cape.

"I haven't evened it out completely," objected Tammy.

"I'll do it myself. I didn't want this much cut off."

"But the split ends were up that high." Tammy shoved her fisted hands onto her ample hips.

"What do I owe?" Shandra wanted out before she lost any more length on her wavy dark hair.

"That's twenty dollars for a trim." Tammy held out her hand.

Shandra dug in her purse and pulled out a twenty. The blow drier shut off. She faced Cecily. "Let me know if there is anything your aunt needs help with."

She didn't wait for a reply. Her legs couldn't carry her fast enough out of the salon. Standing on the street, she spotted a Huckleberry police car cruise by. She'd look up Ryan and see if he wanted to have dinner. She could tell him what she'd learned today.

Walking down Second Street toward the police station, she noticed a woman hurrying toward the back of the medical clinic. There was something familiar about her. The woman glanced up and down the street before entering the building. It was June Hasting.

Chapter Thirteen

What would June be doing slipping in the back door of a medical clinic? It didn't make sense. She stuck that at the back of her mind and continued to the police station. Ryan's Tahoe was parked in front of the building.

The last time she'd set foot in this building, Ryan had placed her in a chair inside the door like a child in time out. She understood now why he'd been upset. She'd barged in on his investigation and he'd nearly shot her. At the time, she'd just thought he was being bossy.

She stepped in the building. A gray-haired woman looked up from a station with phones and radios. She smiled and waved Shandra over.

"You looking for Ryan?"

"Yes, I am." She held out her hand. "Shandra Higheagle."

The woman shook hands. "Pleased to meet you.

I'm Hazel Wells."

"Should I take a seat?" Shandra waved a hand toward the chairs by the door.

"I'll buzz him up, no need to sit unless you've got tired dogs." She picked up the phone and punched in a number. "Ryan, there's someone here for you." She listened and grinned. "He'll be right out."

"Thank you." She'd barely said the words and Ryan appeared in the hallway behind Hazel.

"What are you doing here?" he asked, walking through the half door separating the reception area from the rest of the building.

"I thought we could have dinner before I go home." She didn't want to let the woman know she'd been digging into the murder. It might not look good for Ryan if others knew they worked together.

"I happen to know he skipped lunch," Hazel said. Her eyes twinkled behind the wire-rimmed glasses.

"I'm starving. I didn't have much for breakfast either." Ryan motioned to the door. "Where did you want to go? Ruthie's?"

"No, I was thinking Rigatoni's."

"That's an excellent choice," Hazel said, raising her voice for them to hear as they walked out the door.

"Hazel seems like a nice lady," Shandra said, falling into step beside Ryan.

"She is. She knows a lot about people who live in Huckleberry." Ryan stopped. "Walk or ride?"

"There won't be many more days to be able to walk without freezing. I say walk." Shandra headed back toward Second Street and stopped at the corner. She stared at the medical clinic.

"Why are you staring at the clinic so hard?" Ryan

asked.

"I saw June Hasting go in through a back door when I walked to the police station." She studied Ryan. "Why would she go in the back door? As far as I know she doesn't work there."

"That's the Hasting's pickup. We could wait and ask her." Ryan pointed to an older Chevy pickup parked across the street from the clinic. "It could have something to do with the fact she's pregnant."

Shandra faced Ryan. "How do you know that?"

"Red told me. And it isn't his."

The frown marring Ryan's good looks made her even more curious. "Why did he tell you?"

"He knew his wife and Randal were fooling around. Turns out the deceased gave June something she's wanted for a long time—a baby."

Shandra wrapped her mind around the information. "Just her sleeping around would be motive enough for Red to want to kill J.W. Knowing his wife carried another man's—a rich other man's baby…" She grabbed his sleeve. "Red has to have killed J.W. to keep the man from claiming the child."

"But Red has a solid alibi. He was working in the house. Vivian and Cecily both vouched for his being in the house." Ryan tugged on her arm, turning her down Second Street.

Shandra linked her arm in his. "But they could both be covering for him. We don't know that he didn't sneak out and shoot him at night."

They turned left on Huckleberry.

"I've got a deputy gathering the wildlife cameras. I don't think the ones from the other spots will tell us much, but we'll know the makes and models and know when we find the one that was removed from the murder site."

They continued to the end of the block. Rigatoni's sat on the corner of the last block of town. It was the first restaurant tourists staying at the resort or the motels between town and the ski area saw when driving into Huckleberry.

Ryan held the door, allowing Shandra to enter first.

"Shandra! You haven't been in here in ages." Miranda Adduci, the daughter of the couple who owned the restaurant, gave her a hug.

"Hi Miranda. How are your folks?" The first time Shandra ate at the restaurant the whole family came out of the kitchen to meet her. She'd discovered since, they greet all newcomers to Huckleberry the same way. And from then on treated them like family.

"They are well. Both are in the kitchen tonight. My brother is at the school for a parent's night." Miranda's gaze landed on Ryan. "And I see you have a handsome guest tonight."

"Ryan Greer, this is Miranda Adduci. Her family owns Rigatoni's." Shandra stepped back so Miranda could go in for her usual hug.

Shandra giggled at Ryan's stiffness. Miranda was what some considered a plus size. She was a tall, voluptuous package with a beautiful face and angelic smile. Shandra had bonded with the woman the first time she entered the restaurant.

"Come, I have the perfect table for you two. Quiet, dark, intimate." She winked at Shandra over her shoulder.

Ryan touched her arm. "Are you this friendly with

everyone in Huckleberry?"

"It's a small place with friendly people."

Miranda stopped at a table set for two. It had a view of Huckleberry Mountain.

"This is nice. Thank you." Shandra started to remove her jacket.

Ryan stepped behind her, taking her jacket and pulling her chair out.

She tried to remember the last time she'd been treated like this. Senior prom. Hard to believe the starry-eyed date nearly fifteen years ago was the last time a male she'd dated had treated her with respect.

Ryan handed his coat and her jacket to Miranda.

"Will you be having wine tonight?" she asked.

"Not for me. Shandra?" Ryan settled onto the chair opposite her.

"I have to drive. Not tonight, but I'd love a cup of hot green tea."

"Coffee, please," Ryan said, smiling at their hostess.

Miranda hustled off with the coats and their beverage order.

Ryan studied Shandra. He was surprised to see her on a first name basis with the hostess of the restaurant. He'd thought of her as a hermit, working up at her studio and only coming down to civilization when she had to retrieve supplies.

"I'm glad you brought me here. I'm learning another side of you."

She smiled. "I like people." She scanned the restaurant. "Especially genuine people. The Adducis are so warm and caring. It's hard not to like them."

Miranda arrived with their drinks. "Have you looked at the menu?"

"No, we haven't." Ryan picked up the menu from the table and asked, "What's good here?"

"Everything." Shandra didn't even open the menu. "Why don't you give us whatever the special is?"

"Very good choice. It is Poppa's special dish." Miranda hurried back to the kitchen.

Ryan put the menu down. "You didn't even ask her what it was. How do you know we'll like it?"

"I have yet to eat something here I didn't like." Shandra dunked the tea bag in her tea twice then peered across the table at him. "I've been in town learning more about the Randals."

His good mood slipped a notch. Even though deep down he knew her wanting to have dinner with him was a way to talk to him about Randal's murder, he'd hoped she hadn't been investigating.

"That doesn't surprise me." He sipped his coffee. "Who have you been talking to?"

"Ruthie, Naomi and Ted, and then I ran into Cecily in Peggy's Hair Salon." She held her tea cup to her lips and blew across the top.

"You had a hair appointment at the same time as Cecily?" He found that hard to believe.

"No. I saw her enter the salon, and I followed and had my hair trimmed."

"You didn't get your money's worth, it's uneven." He'd noticed the jagged edges when he'd walked down the hall toward her at the station.

She humphed. "That's another story. I'll have to straighten it out myself tonight."

"What information did you collect?" Ryan didn't

want to encourage her involvement but he'd learned from previous murders in Huckleberry, there was no way to stop her. If he knew what she knew and who she talked with, he had a better chance of keeping her from harm.

"Neither Ruthie nor Ted and Naomi think Vivian killed J.W. Though Ruthie doesn't really know her that well. However, she's heard June talking about J.W. and Vivian." She tapped her chin with a long finger. "With what you told me about June and J.W., I'm wondering if Miss Complainer could have knocked off J.W. when he refused to leave his wife. Maybe she was hoping to become the next Mrs. J.W. Randal."

"But what about her husband? Red." Ryan enjoyed hearing how Shandra's brain operated. It was out of the box and different from his own analytical approach to life and his job.

"I'm thinking June's attempt to get a divorce backfired from your comment Red knows about the baby and was trying to ruin J.W. financially. He'd never give up June from the sounds of things."

"Following that logic, June should have shot Red." Ryan smiled at the narrowing of Shandra's golden eyes.

"That's true. I think we can rule out June. The first person she'd have to get rid of would have been her husband. But what if she and Red planned for her to get pregnant by J.W. hoping to collect money to keep it quiet?" Her eyes lit up at her newfound reasoning.

"Then why would Red try to ruin J.W. financially?"

Ryan leaned back, ending the conversation as the hostess delivered their salads. "Thank you."

Shandra stabbed at the lettuce. "Why would June be going in the back door of the clinic? Do you think she is hiding the pregnancy? If so, why? Her husband knows. Anyone would think it is Red's baby."

"I don't know. I might be able to check on that tomorrow. What did you learn from Cecily?" Ryan started on his salad. His mouth watered at the freshness of the greens and the herbs in the dressing. One thing he'd learned about Shandra, she did have a talent for knowing good food.

"Cicely didn't care for her uncle. She made the comment he put his hands down every woman's pants. You could tell it upset her." Shandra held a forkful of salad between her mouth and the plate.

"Takagi told me he witnessed J.W. being handsie with Cecily behind the house."

She set the fork down forcefully. "I don't think it was consensual. There was too much disgust on her face when she said it." She shoved the salad to the middle of the table. "Might be a good idea to look into other women he came on to."

"This topic is ruining your appetite. Let's change the subject." Ryan finished his salad and placed her plate on top of his. "Have you decided on your clothing for Conor's wedding?"

"Yes. Why do you care?" She smiled.

"I'd like to buy you a corsage but need to know what color would go with your clothing." He hadn't been as excited to take a girl or woman on a date since his junior prom.

"That's sweet! But I don't want to be thought of as part of the family." Her gaze dropped to the table cloth were she fiddled with her silverware.

"Why not? I'm the best man so it would only be fitting for you to be considered part of the wedding party." He didn't like her feeling she shouldn't be included. She was his date and his mother and sisters would never forgive him if he didn't include Shandra in all the wedding activities, including the rehearsal dinner the night before. A small thing he hadn't mentioned to her yet.

"You are very open minded, and I'm sure your family is too, but I was taught from an early age to keep my Nez Perce side hidden and not to get too familiar with people. My mother constantly told me you don't know how people will really act until it's too late." She raised her chin and peered into his eyes. "You don't care about my heritage, but if someone in your family does, I don't want to ruin your day with your family."

Ryan reached across the table palm up. Hesitantly, she placed her hand in his. "If I bring you to the wedding and introduce you as my friend, everyone in my family will include you and every man at the wedding will wish they were me." He squeezed her hand. "You'll be surprised to see you won't be the only Native American there. I told you about my friend in school. His brother was good friends with Conor."

Miranda returned with their meal. One whiff and Ryan's stomach gurgled with happiness.

"Poppa's chicken cacciatore. Enjoy." Miranda took away the salad plates and disappeared.

"This looks delicious." He shoved his fork into the dish and spun the utensil, capturing the pasta.

"I'm wearing a colorful tunic and brown leggings. You said the wedding was outside and casual." She took a bite of the dish. Her eyes closed.

He understood her reverence to the food. His mother had never made anything this good. "I'm glad you suggested this place. It beats burgers."

They finished their meal with small talk.

Miranda arrived carrying two small plates with a thinly-layered dessert. "These are on the house."

"I love tiramisu!" Shandra said, licking her lips as Miranda placed a dessert in front of her.

Ryan locked that away for future reference. "I don't believe I've had this before." He dipped his fork into the fluffy dessert and savored the bite. "Wow. This is good."

They finished the desserts along with another cup of coffee and tea.

Miranda was bringing their coats to them when raised voices floated back to their corner.

Chapter Fourteen

Shandra recognized the voices that were arguing loudly. She glanced over her shoulder at Ryan as he helped her on with her coat. "Recognize the voices?"

He nodded and led her toward the front of the restaurant.

Red and June Hasting sat at a table not far from the door. Both had stormy faces and their arms crossed. Obviously, they'd come to a standoff about something.

"Do we say hello?" Shandra asked.

Ryan didn't answer, merely walked over to the table. "Good evening, Mr. and Mrs. Hasting. Are you celebrating something?"

The two couldn't have missed the innuendo in his comment.

Red shoved up from the table. "What are you insinuating?"

"Nothing. This is a nice restaurant with a lovely atmosphere. Just the kind of place to go for a celebration. That's all." He grasped Shandra's hand, leading her out of the building.

"What was that all about?" Shandra asked, as Ryan led her across the street and around the corner.

He stopped. "I just want to see what they do now."

"They had food sitting on the table. They'll eat." She pulled her jacket around her tighter and peeked around his shoulder.

Ryan put an arm around her, drawing her close to him as they both watched the Hastings through the restaurant window.

June wasn't eating. She shoved her plate to the middle of the table and hurried toward the restrooms. Red threw his napkin onto his plate and stared after her.

Shandra pushed closer to Ryan to stave off the cold settling over the town. "She's taking a long time in the restroom."

"Too long." Ryan rubbed his hand up and down her arm.

"Do you think she went out the back to avoid a confrontation with her husband?" Shandra could see the timid woman doing just that.

June didn't return after ten minutes. Red went to the restrooms and returned within minutes. He grabbed their coats from the backs of their chairs and shoved out the front doors.

"Come on. Let's see if June left the pickup by the clinic." Ryan captured her hand, and they turned to walk down Second Street.

Someone stepped out of the alley that ran behind the businesses alongside Rigatoni's.

"That has to be June," Shandra whispered and hastened her steps.

"Not too fast. We don't want to scare her. Act natural." Ryan slowed their pace and walked along as if they were on a stroll.

June reached the pickup and dug in her purse for her keys.

An old jeep revved up the street and screeched to a halt beside the pickup. The door flung open and Red emerged. He shook June's coat at her as he approached.

"We need to do something." Shandra's stomach churned with worry for the woman.

"If he gets physical I will. I need to see if his professed love is true." Ryan leaned into the shadow of a building, drawing her with him.

"I can't believe you won't talk to me about this!" Red advanced on June but only held her coat out to her.

"There's nothing to talk about. I made a mistake. I'm taking care of the mistake." June's flat tone scared Shandra more than Red's aggressiveness. It was as if she'd given up on life.

"What do you mean taking care of the mistake?" Red looked across the street. "Why are you parked near the clinic? You said you were meeting your sister this afternoon." He stared at his wife. "Did you meet her here? Why didn't you bring me to your doctor's appointment?"

"Because I didn't want you to know about it. Red, I can't have this baby. Not now." June dropped her face into her hands and started crying. Her shoulders shook.

Shandra's heart went out to the woman.

"What do you mean you can't have the baby? You've wanted a baby since we first married." Red stepped forward, his arms extended as if to take her into them.

June backed away. "I slept with another man. I thought I loved him and he loved me. I can't be your wife, and I can't take care of a baby on my own. I made an appointment to have a—a…"

"No! I won't have you take a life. You'll regret it. You won't be able to live with a decision like that." Red did take her in his arms this time. He held his wife as she cried.

Shandra tugged on Ryan's sleeve. "I think this is something we shouldn't have seen."

He nodded and followed her back to Huckleberry Street.

"Where are you parked?" Ryan asked, his tone somber.

"By Ruthie's." She wrapped her arms around her body. "My mother was pregnant with me before she married Daddy. When he found out he insisted they marry."

"You say that like it's a puzzle." Ryan put an arm around her shoulders.

"Mother never told me that little detail. I learned it from Phil Seeton, the old man who rodeoed with my father." Phil had told her other things that had kept her awake nights and searching the internet.

"I'm glad your mother didn't contemplate what it sounds like June Hasting is." Ryan kissed her temple.

"I'm not so sure she wouldn't have aborted me if Daddy hadn't stepped in. I'm the cause of her being married to an Indian and suffering ridicule for five years." Shandra shivered. She wasn't sure if it was from the cold or the realization her mother might have ended her life to keep from being married to her father.

"You need to go home and get a good night's sleep. I have more suspects to visit with tomorrow." Ryan stopped beside her Jeep.

"Who?" She needed to take her mind off the image of June that shifted into her mother.

"Todd Smith, who helped Randal set-up the wildlife cameras, and Melvin Clower, the Fish and Game officer who handled the arrests and paperwork on the illegal tag infractions." Ryan held out his hand for her keys.

She handed them over. "What about Cecily's accusations about J.W. putting his hands down any female's pants? And his attention to her? You going to look into others he might have been sleeping with?"

Ryan unlocked her door, handed her the keys, and helped her into the driver's seat. "I'll check that out if other names come up. Right now, no one else has been linked to J.W.

"I also have to go through the SD cards from the wildlife cameras and see if I can find out which one is missing. The killer may still have it or tried to take it to a pawn shop." Ryan placed a hand on her cheek. "Don't dwell on the past. I see a bright, happy future for you."

Staring into his eyes, she could see a happy future too, but her curiosity about the past needed to be satisfied.

She put her hand over his. "I'll only dwell on what will heal my heart. Good-night." She grasped his hand, squeezed, and let him go. Closing the vehicle door, she blew him a kiss and started up the Jeep. Ryan stood in the street watching her until she drove out of town.

The drive home only brought up more questions.

The one that nagged at her the most was Cecily's disgust of her uncle. If he'd made a pass at her, did he have a penchant for younger girls? How do I find out if he's had contact with other young girls?

All the lights were blazing as she pulled up to her house. Sheba bounded out from behind the barn. Proving she'd been keeping Lil company. Thankful for Lil, she walked up a well-lit walkway and into a warm, bright house.

Now that she no longer had to drive, she headed to the kitchen and poured a glass of wine. Sheba stretched out in front of the couch.

"This is where you think I should drink my wine?" she asked, hitting the remote and turning on the gas fireplace. Shandra settled onto the couch and tried to think of something other than the troubling thoughts that had hounded her on the drive.

The warmth and wine made her eyelids heavy. She drifted into a dream.

"Ella, what are you doing here?" she questioned her grandmother. The old woman beckoned her closer. They were in the forest, hidden behind a large pine tree. Peeking around the trunk of the tree, Shandra watched a man with his back to her, open what looked like a camera and put the SD card in an electronic tablet. The man swore, yanked the SD card out of the tablet, and smashed it into the ground. He replaced the camera and stormed off. "Who is he, Ella?" she asked. But her grandmother was gone. The spot where he'd stomped on the SD card had a light shining down on it. She wasn't familiar with the area. But could tell it wasn't where Ryan claimed the body had been shot.

Chapter Fifteen

Ryan spent the next morning playing phone tag to make appointments with Todd Smith and Melvin Clower. While he was on the phone, Deputy Speaks arrived at the police station.

"Did you find anything interesting at the murder site?" Ryan asked, leaning back in the chair and taking a sip of the coffee Hazel had placed beside the keyboard fifteen minutes earlier.

"We found the bullet in a tree about thirty feet from the shell casing. Thirty-aught-six. Like Rickman said." Speaks pulled up a chair.

Hazel appeared with a cup of coffee for him and heated up Ryan's.

"Thanks Hazel. You don't need to wait on us," Ryan said.

"It's the only way I can eavesdrop." The woman winked and went back to her station.

Ryan laughed. Speaks just stared at the woman.

"She won't tell anyone what we say. She's my encyclopedia of the people who live in Huckleberry." Ryan picked up the report Speaks set on the desk.

He read through the preliminary report. "You found evidence of three different-sized footprints?" Ryan set the report down. "All male?"

"Hard to tell. They were all hiking-type boots. Three different sizes. One could have been a woman with a big foot or a man with a small foot." Speaks took a sip of the coffee. "Not bad."

"Just don't take any the chief offers you." Ryan clicked off the male suspects in his mind. So far none of them had smallish feet. "Did they match one set to the deceased?"

"Yes. We never did find a camera." Speaks grabbed the cell phone in his breast pocket, glanced at the number, and stood. "I need to take this."

Ryan's phone rang. "Detective Greer."

"This is Melvin Clower. I heard you wanted to talk with me."

"Yes. Is there a time and place we can meet?"

"I'll be at the Fish and Game office this afternoon." He paused. "What is this about?"

"The allegations against J.W. Randal." Ryan wasn't going to say anything about the man being dead if the Fish and Game officer didn't know.

"Do you think that had anything to do with his death?"

The hopefulness in the man's voice raised Ryan's interest. "That's what I'm trying to determine."

"I'll be at the Fish and Game office at one." Ryan pushed the off button and started to redial Todd Smith.

His phone buzzed. "Detective Greer," he answered

without looking at the number.

"I had a dream last night," Shandra said without so much as a greeting.

The breathiness of her voice told him she believed the dream might have something to do with the murder.

"What was it about?" He never wrote down her dreams or how they led him to clues. There were very few law enforcement colleagues who believed in psychic help when it came to catching murderers. However, Ryan grew up being told of the little people from his Irish mother and had Native American friends who told him stories he believed. All his past experience made him a believer in Shandra's dreams even when she wasn't.

"A man in the forest pulled an SD card out of a camera and stomped it into the ground." Her voice shook with anticipation. "Do you have the locations of the wildlife cameras on Randal's property?"

"I do have the information. Why?" He knew where this was leading and didn't like the idea of her traipsing around in the forest.

"I think I can find the spot if I visit the locations. I know it wasn't where we found the dead elk. The trees were larger, the undergrowth denser."

"You think the SD card will still be on the ground?" The whole idea was as farfetched as believing in her dreams.

"Yes. Lil and I can scout around and see if I can find it." Shandra had to make Ryan see this was the best way to get information that would help the investigation.

She bit her lip. He had to agree. As usual, talking to

Ryan about a dream made it feel less hokey and more real. Even though all the dreams where Ella appeared had proven to be viable clues, she still questioned her sanity upon waking.

"I won't have you going onto Randal's property. That would be trespassing. If you can wait until later this afternoon, I'll bring the map and we'll decide which places to look tomorrow."

"But tomorrow—"

Ryan cut her off. "It will be too late by the time I finish my interviews today to ride around on the mountain looking for specific areas."

Disappointment lodged in her chest. She'd hoped to have the clue in her hands by this evening. Without the knowledge of the camera sites she'd be wandering around the forest like a blind person.

She opened the paper Lil had picked up with the mail earlier that morning. There was a front-page article on the death of J.W. Randal.

"Okay. I'll wait for you to bring the information." Shandra pressed the off button and started reading the small town bias of J.W.'s life.

She read the article and reread it to make sure she didn't miss anything that might be a clue to who would want him dead. The main thing that stuck out was the fact that J.W. and his wife moved to Huckleberry five years ago. And while the wife was a prominent figure in all the local charities and fundraisers, J.W. had made more enemies than friends. He was brash and loud spoken, and then the illegal hunting on Huckleberry Mountain had turned just about every local against him. The mountain and the wildlife were part of the draw for tourists. And tourism was the main thing that kept the little community from becoming a ghost town. The article mentioned how an anonymous tip was turned in to Fish and Game about his illegal hunting methods. A long-time resident and Fish and Game officer Melvin Clower was sent to investigate.

She sucked in air reading the part about how Randal's neighbor, local artist Shandra Higheagle, had found the body on her property. And how it seemed that once again the artist found herself in the middle of a murder investigation.

"Now mother will see this," Shandra said, petting Sheba's head. "That's all I need."

She set the paper down and closed her eyes to resurrect the images from her dream. If she didn't think about it long and hard, she'd forget the details that would help her find the SD card.

Sheba bumped her arm.

"Yes, you want to go for a walk. So do I." Shandra glanced down at the paper. "I think we should take a neighborly stroll over to the Randals with a sympathy card. I need to figure out if that blue-crystal pendant we found belongs to one of the women on the Randal property."

Shandra dressed, fed Sheba, and ate a couple slices of toast. She picked out one of the watercolor cards she painted when drawing up vase designs. She added her condolences and signed it.

Outside, the crisp air filled her lungs. Soon October would be here and the leaves would turn colors, drift to the ground, and crunch underfoot. She loved the fall. The need for sweaters and sweatshirts and the sense of the world around her hibernating.

A few more days and she'd be traveling north to the wedding with Ryan. She was curious about his family. She'd witnessed his annoyance and love for his sisters. When he talked about his siblings and parents, she could feel the closeness. That was something she had never felt with her mother and step-father. It was as if they kept her at arm's length, never wanting to get close. She believed her mother loved her but was almost afraid to show it.

Shandra walked into the barn.

"Where are you going so early? I thought you wanted to work in the studio today." Lil, her conscience, stood just outside the door to the tack room where she lived.

Try as she might to get the woman to move into the house, or into the small apartment above the studio, Lil adamantly declined and resided in the tack room, using the small bathroom in the upstairs apartment.

"Taking a sympathy card to Vivian Randal." Shandra tucked the card into her down vest pocket and grabbed Apple's bridle.

"You could mail it. Or better yet, wait until Detective Greer can go with you." Lil followed her to the corral.

"I'll just drop it off—"

"And get in trouble somehow."

Shandra made a face at Lil. "How can I get into trouble by dropping off a sympathy card?"

"You'll ask questions that will make them think you're trying to find the killer, which you are, and then Detective Greer will have to save you, again." Lil had her arms crossed over her extra-large purple sweatshirt. Her spiky hair stuck out underneath a purple stocking cap.

"What if I said, I'd love to have you join me?" Shandra hoped the woman's protectiveness and curiosity would get her a riding partner.

"They don't want me over there." Lil shook her head.

"You don't have to come in the house. You can wait outside with the horses if you're uncomfortable." Shandra didn't believe Vivian or Cecily were dangerous and after last night she doubted the Hastings were either, but she'd learned after the last two bodies she'd found to never trust anyone. The only people she trusted and knew didn't kill J.W. were Ryan and Lil.

The woman nodded her head and walked over to her horse's stall.

Within minutes Apple and Sunshine, Lil's horse, were saddled, and they headed down the lane with Sheba trotting ahead.

Going straight through the forest to the hidden gate would have been quicker, but Shandra didn't want to make a habit of using the gate or messing up anything that might be evidence.

At the Randal's driveway the gates were shut.

"Looks like they don't want company," Lil commented. She reined Sunshine around.

"I'm sure they don't mean well-meaning neighbors." Shandra dismounted and opened the gate, waving Lil through.

"Didn't they have gates in Montana?" Lil asked.

"They did. But neighbors were neighborly." Shandra re-mounted and continued up the driveway.

Fifty feet from the house they stopped the horses as

Red walked out the front door. "Didn't you see the closed gate? This family is grieving."

Shandra walked Apple up to the walkway. "I came to deliver a sympathy card." She dismounted, handed the reins to Lil, and told Sheba to stay.

Red took a couple steps forward. "Thank you, now leave. Viv—Mrs. Randal isn't in the mood for visitors." He took the card Shandra extended.

"Please let her know if there is anything I can do for her, all she has to do is ask. Neighbors should be there for one another." Shandra stayed where she was hoping the man would give in at her sincerity.

"Viv—Mrs. Randal has her niece. She'll be fine." Red turned, dismissing her.

"Please relay my willingness to help with anything." Shandra huffed when the man entered the house and closed the door soundly.

"Told you so," Lil said, holding out Apple's reins.

Shandra couldn't stop the smile creeping onto her lips. "Yes, you did."

She swung up into the saddle and turned Apple back down the driveway. Once she was out of sight of the house, she turned into the trees.

"Where are you going?" Lil asked, stopping her horse on the road.

"I don't feel like opening and closing that gate. Let's just cut through the forest." Shandra kept going, knowing Lil would follow. She was too protective to leave her loose in the woods.

Chapter Sixteen

Ryan decided that since he couldn't contact Todd Smith via phone he'd drive to Hafersville and see if he could catch up to the man. He seemed to be a one-man security outfit. There was an answering machine at his business number and his cell phone said his inbox was full.

The drive took him past Shandra and the Randal's driveways. The closed gate at the Randal driveway raised his suspicions. If there had been media trying to get in it would make sense but there wasn't a soul stopped on the road hoping to get in and speak to the family. Why were they closing out the rest of the world? Especially when they know the police will have to speak to them about the investigation.

If he hadn't set his mind on contacting Smith, he would have turned around and entered those closed gates. Something was up.

Forty minutes later, he found the small building

two blocks off Main Street where Smith had his office. The building was dark, but he tried the door anyway. It gave and he walked in. A red blinking light shone up by the ceiling across from the door. He had surveillance cameras.

"Todd Smith, I'm with the Weippe County Sheriff's Office," he said loud enough for any receivers to pick up his voice.

The lights came on and a door directly under the surveillance camera opened.

"What brings the county to my door?" asked a small, bald-headed man between fifty and sixty.

"I'm investigating the murder of J.W. Randal." Ryan showed the man his badge.

"I saw the story in the paper. Didn't believe it at first. J.W. was one tough hombre." Smith closed the door behind him and leaned against a glass counter filled with wildlife and surveillance cameras.

"I understand you helped him install wildlife cameras on his property." Ryan pulled out his notepad and pen.

"Yes, what does that have to do with his murder?" Smith straightened.

"One of the cameras is missing. The one where we believe he was shot." Ryan studied the man. He didn't show any nervous ticks or tendencies. His hands remained steady, his gaze didn't flicker.

Smith rubbed a hand over his bald head. "Which camera?"

"That's what I'm hoping you can tell me. I have the serial numbers of the others. We need you to check your records to find the missing serial number. If whoever took it tries to sell or pawn the camera, we can hopefully catch them and ask why, and see if they are the murderer." Ryan flipped open his notepad to the page with the serial numbers Speaks gave him that morning.

"Sure. I have the serial numbers and the areas they were each set up." Smith turned to the door. "I'll be right back. I keep all the paperwork in the back. People don't like knowing someone is watching them." He disappeared.

Ryan wasn't worried he wouldn't return. The man hadn't shown any worried or fearful actions. He seemed willing to help.

Smith returned with a notebook. The side had the word RANDAL written in black marker.

"I keep a notebook on all clients. The equipment they purchase and where it's located on their property or on the property of the person they are spying on. When the subpoenas come in from spouses and the like, it makes my life a whole lot easier to just hand over the notebook."

He handed the book to Ryan.

There were only six pages in the inch-wide binder. Ryan scanned the serial numbers matching them to the ones on his notepad. He placed a finger on the third one. "That's the missing camera." He scribbled the number in his pad.

Smith turned the book his way. "Six, zero, three." He turned the page and skimmed his finger down the page. "Here. That camera was set up about fifty feet from the fence line of his neighbor on the east side. It was attached to a tree four feet from the ground. He wanted to see if there was a pattern in the movement of the elk coming across the fence at that point."

"How easy would that camera be to spot?"

"They were cameras to watch wildlife. They weren't hidden at all."

"Anyone could have spotted the camera and yanked it off the tree?" Was the camera yanked off before or after the murder? If the person knew of the camera, he would have removed it before killing the man. If he spotted it afterward, he would have yanked it off to hide evidence of the crime.

"It was in plain sight. J.W. wanted it that way so his employee could find them easily to remove the SD cards for viewing."

Ryan pulled the book back toward him and scanned the pages. *New SD card installed in camera 5.* It was a handwritten notation.

"What's this about?" He asked.

Smith read the notation and shook his head. "Red Hasting called me and said he thought he forgot to put a new SD card into camera five but he didn't have any extras so could I send them a new one."

"When was this?" Ryan had a feeling he knew where the missing SD card was.

"About three weeks ago."

Ryan made a notation of *camera 5-find location* in his notepad. "Thank you for your help. I'll need to take that book as evidence." He packed the book out to his SUV, pulled out an evidence bag and filled out the information. Then he took a form back to Smith and had him sign that the book had been in his possession and he released it to Detective Greer with the time and date.

Ryan shook Smith's hand. "If you happen to think

of anything that might be of help, give me a call." He handed the man a card with his name and number.

Sliding into the driver's seat, Ryan glanced at the clock on his dash. He barely had time to get back to Huckleberry in an hour to interview Clower.

~*~

Shandra led Lil through the trees and around behind the Randal buildings.

"This isn't the way to your fence. In fact, it's the complete opposite," Lil said, in a voice louder than was necessary.

"You want to get us caught?" Shandra whispered loudly.

"I'm trying to keep you from getting arrested for trespassing." Again, her voice was too loud.

"Shhh. I'm looking for the start of the path that goes to the hidden gate I found the other day." Shandra knew exactly where the path started. It started at the back of the Randal barn. The barn that housed the surveillance equipment according to Ryan. She was determined to find out the locations of the cameras. She was confident the dream Ella sent to her would help them find J.W.'s killer.

"I can see it plain as day over there." Lil pointed to their left.

Shandra sent one long look at the back of the barn and turned Apple onto the trail. Maybe bringing Lil along hadn't been such a good idea. Having a conscience with a loud voice wasn't as easy to ignore as the tiny one sitting on her shoulder.

With a deep sigh, she continued up the trail. Lil didn't say a thing, and Sheba bounded up the trail in front of them.

Shandra lost sight of her dog as her mind raced back over the scene at the Randal house. She couldn't come up with any reason why they would shut the world out. Not unless one of them had confessed to killing J.W. and the rest were rallying around to keep the secret.

"Woof! Woof!" Sheba's surprised bark echoed through the forest.

Shandra turned in her saddle and glanced back at Lil. She shrugged.

Urging Apple into a trot, she hurried forward to see what had startled Sheba.

The dog had reached the hidden gate. Three men in deputy uniforms were backed against the fence staring at Sheba.

"Down girl," Shandra said, just to put the men at ease. Within minutes of recognizing her master was close to protect her, Sheba loped up to the men. Whimpering and squirming like a puppy, she licked each one on the back of their hand before trotting back to Shandra.

She recognized one man as one of the two deputies who had first arrived when Ryan called in the body.

"Miss Higheagle what are you doing on the Randal's property?" the deputy asked, stepping away from the other men. She read his name tag. Trapp.

"Lil and I delivered a sympathy card," she said, feeling no guilt at being caught.

"You could have used the road," he countered.

"We could have. But it won't be long and we won't be able to go on a horse ride because of all the snow."

"I realize you are the one who reported this gate.

But do you think it's wise to use it right now?" Deputy Trapp now stood beside Apple's head. He grasped the headstall.

"Whoever killed my neighbor isn't interested in me." She stared at his hand wrapped around the leather headstall. "Please release my horse and let us through." Her voice came out harder and deeper than she'd intended.

The man's eyes widened then narrowed. "I'll tell you when you can go."

The beeping of a phone being dialed chimed. The sound came across as absurd in the middle of the forest.

Deputy Trapp released Apple and strode toward Lil. "What are you doing?"

"Calling Detective Greer to tell him you're detaining us," Lil said, staring at the man.

Over the years Shandra had gotten used to Lil's deadpan delivery of information. It was apparent her delivery came across as sarcastic to the deputy.

He tried to swipe the phone out of Lil's hands. Sunshine, a mare who'd been with Lil for twenty years, backed up, moving her owner out of harm's way.

Sheba also bounded into the mix and soon there was man, horse and rider, and dog swirling together.

Shandra called and whistled trying to capture Sheba's attention. From the sparkle in her eyes and tongue hanging out, she thought the man and horse and rider were playing a game.

Fear stabbed her chest when Sunshine tripped and Lil nearly came unseated.

"Stop!" Shandra yelled. The sound echoed through the trees, startling everyone.

The commotion halted.

"Lil won't call Detective Greer. But you have no right to detain us." Shandra urged Apple over next to Sunshine. She directed her attention to the men at the gate. "Would you please move so we can pass through and get back home?"

The men moved. She waved Lil to go first. Once Lil and Sheba were on her property, Shandra turned to Deputy Trapp. "I'll not say anything about this to Detective Greer. But if I see you on my property after this investigation is over, I'll turn you in for harassment." She urged Apple into a trot and caught up to Lil.

"That's one little rooster who has to prove he's worthy of the badge," Lil said.

"You think that's all it was? I felt more animosity than that." Shandra glanced over her shoulder even though they were out of sight of the fence line.

"Maybe. Why did you insist on coming that way?"

"I wanted to see if they would be investigating that section of fence. Ryan didn't think it had anything to do with the murder, but from the looks of things, he is having the whole fence line checked out." I wonder if the SD card came from a camera along the fence line? If so, they're heading downhill…

Chapter Seventeen

Ryan pulled up in front of the Fish and Game office fifteen minutes after one. He'd tried to return in time, but on the way back he'd come across an elderly lady sitting alongside the road with a flat tire. He'd stopped to change her tire, making him late for his meeting with Clower.

He pushed through the doors of the building straight into the same bustle as the day before.

"Good afternoon, detective. Melvin is waiting for you down the hall, second door to the left," the receptionist said, before picking up the ringing telephone.

Ryan thanked her and headed down the hall. He knocked on the second door to the left.

"Come in."

He opened the door and found a desk covered with

files, an old computer monitor, and a man dressed in the gray and green fish and game uniform.

"You must be Detective Greer." Clower stood and extended a hand over the desk.

"I am. Mr. Clower, thank you for making time for me." Ryan shook hands and took a seat in front of the desk.

"No problem. I've never had a person I've been investigating come up dead." Clower sat behind the desk, shuffled stacks of files around, and avoided eye contact.

"What evidence did you have against him?" Ryan had read what he could attain at the courthouse but that was mostly legal jargon. He wanted the Fish and Game officer to give him his informal view of the investigation.

"His employee, Red Hasting, tipped us to the illegal activities. I have his affidavit. With that I was able to get a warrant and seize his records. The man had been purchasing tags under his employee's and family's names for years and then selling them along with hunting privileges. Some of the animals were poached or shot out of season."

"How did he, or for that matter, his clients, get away with shooting out of season? The taxidermist would have known." Ryan didn't like the idea of yet another person who could have been implicated in the illegal hunting and took revenge.

"Turns out Randal had a cousin who was a taxidermist. He did the jobs on the off-season animals claiming the hides had been frozen to give him an income when the work was slower." Clower rolled his eyes, insinuating he knew the man was lying.

"Was the cousin upset Randal had been caught and he was fingered?" Ryan pulled out his notepad and poised his pen over a blank page getting ready to jot down the cousin's name.

"No. The cousin adamantly said he didn't know the animals were poached or that J.W. was using illegal tags. When I asked him how he accounted for the fact people other than J.W. paid him for the jobs, he said they didn't. J.W. paid for the mounts. Which means the mount fees were paid by the hunters directly to J.W. Going over his records, he charged them double the cost his cousin charged him."

"The cousin wouldn't have any reason to kill J.W., unless you told him about the higher charge." He watched Clower.

"I didn't say a word. Figured when the information came out he'd discover he was being used then, but I wasn't going to tell him." Clower leaned back, placing his locked fingers behind his head. "You looking for someone in my investigation that might have had a beef with Randal?"

"I was hoping you could lead me toward a good suspect." Ryan placed his notepad on his knee.

"The only person I came across in the investigation who appeared mad enough to kill the guy was his wife." Clower leaned forward. "Everyone told me that woman was quiet and meek. When I went to their house to get the records and she heard what I was there about, she lit into him like a rabid cougar. She was hissing and spitting. Some of the things she was saying didn't make much sense. But I can tell you, he went stone cold when she said she'd ignored his fling with June, but raking their names through the mud with illegal hunting she wouldn't stand for."

Ryan sat up. "She told him she knew of his affair with their hired help? Was Red present?"

"Red, June, that niece. They all heard her lay into J.W." He shook his head. "The disgusting part? He admitted it to her and the whole lot of them. Turned the table on Mrs. Randal, telling her she was worthless as a woman and deriding her something awful. Red stepped in and told him to shut his mouth." Clower tapped a finger against the desk top. "That man was sticking up for Mrs. Randal like he had a thing for her. And right after hearing Randal say he'd been sleeping with his wife." He ran a hand over his face. "That whole house was confusing. But by the looks on all their faces…anyone of them could have shot Randal."

"Would you say the people on that property would have had more reason than anyone you came across in your investigations?" Ryan liked the idea of localizing his search to the inhabitants of the Randal property.

"The people he involved in the illegal hunting were pissed, but they all wrote it off as bad business. None of them that I could tell took it personally." Clower picked up a fat file on the right side of his desk. "I can have copies of my investigation sent to you or you can wait while I copy them."

"If you don't mind, I'll wait while you copy them." Ryan settled back in the chair.

"I'll give these to Janet and get us a cup of coffee." Clower left the room.

Ryan took this time to look around. He spotted a picture frame hidden among the stacks of files Clower had shuffled around. Judging from the position of the files and photo, he'd tried to hide the photo. Ryan pulled the five-by-seven frame out from between the stacks. It was Clower, a dark-haired woman about Clower's age, and a teenage girl with a close resemblance to the older woman, smiling for the camera. The setting behind them looked like a fair.

The door opened and the smell of coffee entered the room followed by Clower carrying two mugs.

"Nice family," Ryan said, replacing the photo on the desk.

Clower stopped, dropped his gaze to the photo, and looked down at the mugs in his hands. "Thanks." He continued into the room and placed a mug on his desk in front of Ryan. "My wife and daughter. We had someone at the State Fair take that photo for us a month ago."

He took his seat behind the desk. "Janet will be in with your copies in a few minutes."

Clower sipped his coffee. His gaze lingered on the photo. Something in his eyes piqued Ryan's attention.

"How old is your daughter?"

The man's angry gaze leveled on Ryan. "She's seventeen. Too young for you."

Ryan raised his hands as if surrendering. "Hey, I'm not looking. I have a *woman* I'm interested in."

"Sorry. I tend to be overprotective. Or at least that's what my wife tells me." He smiled wanly and took another sip of coffee.

A quick knock and Janet, the receptionist who had greeted Ryan when he arrived, walked in with the folder and a thick manila envelope. "Here you go," she said, placing the file on the desk and handing the envelope to Ryan.

"Thank you." Ryan stood. "Thank you for your time Mr. Clower and the files." He left the room and the building. Something about the visit ticked at his brain but he couldn't put a finger on it.

~*~

Shandra tried to ditch Lil at the barn and head back up the mountain, but the canny woman came up with reasons for Shandra to get into the studio and work. Even with her mind elsewhere, she managed to etch Huckleberry Mountain on four dozen clay coasters the local businesses sold as souvenirs. She'd made so many of them the last two years that etching the mountain had become second nature.

Jazz tunes tinkled from her phone. She wiped her hands and dug the phone out of the breast pocket of the denim shirt she wore over a t-shirt. Ryan.

"Hello," she answered.

"Hey there. I heard you were caught trespassing today."

Shoot! She thought she'd intimidated the deputy enough he wouldn't say anything.

"I wasn't trespassing. I was delivering a sympathy card." She'd stick to that line till she died.

"What did you say to Deputy Trapp? He wouldn't say you had or hadn't been over there, but Scanlon said you and Lil were caught riding on Randal property and heading to the gate you were so angry about yesterday."

She heard the humor in his tone.

"So Trapp didn't say anything?" She had intimidated the man. She didn't know if that made her proud or feel like a bully.

"No, he didn't. Scanlon said you were pretty tough.

But I guess whatever threat you made to Trapp didn't include him."

She laughed. "No I made the threat specifically to Trapp. He didn't need to grab Apple's headstall and go all Dirty Harry on me just for riding home from the neighbors."

Ryan laughed. "Dirty Harry? That's not a nickname I'd give Trapp."

"Did you call to tell me you're bringing the map of the wildlife cameras over?" She'd spent the time etching the coasters reliving the dream. She didn't want to lose the vision and impression of the area where the SD card was shoved into the ground.

"Yes. I'll be there in twenty minutes. Any chance you can whip up something for me to eat? I missed lunch helping a lady change a flat tire." Ryan's voice drifted off wearily.

"I'm sure you were a hero to the woman. Yes, I'll start dinner as soon as you hang up."

The phone went dead. She laughed and headed to the house. Good thing she'd set out salmon steaks that morning. Nothing cooked faster than fish. She started the grill on the way into the house, then washed her hands and prepared a salad while the fish marinated.

Sheba's welcoming bark told her when Ryan pulled up. Shandra carried the fish to the barbeque and placed them on the grill.

Ryan came around the side of the house. His smile was welcoming, his step weary. He carried a file folder.

"You look beat. Want a beer?" Shandra pulled out a chair by the patio table.

"Yes and yes." He plopped into the wicker chair.

Shandra retrieved a beer and her glass of wine. She returned to the patio, handed Ryan the beer, and checked the fish.

"That smells delicious." Ryan twisted the cap off his beer.

"It will be ready in ten minutes. Do you want to eat out here? It's starting to get cool."

"I'll follow you inside when you take the fish." He swallowed the beer and settled into the cushion on the chair.

They didn't say any more while she plucked the fish from the grill, placed it on a platter, and turned off the propane.

Shandra headed into the house with Ryan following. She'd set two places at the counter. Ryan pulled up a stool and took a seat to her right. Shandra placed the platter of fish on the counter next to the salad she'd made and pulled half a loaf of garlic bread out of the oven.

"This looks good and smells delicious." Ryan waited for her to take the stool next to him before dishing food onto his plate.

"Since you know how I spent my day, how did you spend yours?" Shandra asked, placing food on her plate.

"I talked with Smith and Clower. Both had some interesting information. Smith is the man who arranged the wildlife cameras and helped set them up. In his records there is mention of a missing SD card."

Shandra's heart nearly stopped. As much as she believed in her dreams, she still found it hard to completely accept them. "So there really could be a SD card in the ground."

"Yes. Just like you dreamed." Ryan grasped her

hand.

She stared into his eyes. He believed in her dreams. Why can't I fully believe in them?

"Do you know which one? Which camera?" She wouldn't have to ride all over the mountain. They could go to the right spot, and she'd direct them to the area.

"Yes. I know which camera and with the map Hasting gave me we'll know where on the mountain to look." He took a bite of salmon.

Shandra stared at his tired face. "Do you have extra clothes with you?"

His gaze jerked up from his plate and searched her face. "Yes. Why?"

"You can stay in the guest room tonight, and we can ride to the spot in the morning."

A smile twitched his lips. "That's the best offer I've had in a while. I'll take you up on it."

They finished the meal in companionable silence. After the dishes were in the dishwasher, they retired to the living room.

On the sofa, sitting side by side, Ryan pulled out the map and pointed to an area marked with a number five. "That's the area where the SD card went missing."

"That isn't very far from the county road." Shandra pointed to a gray line. "That's an old forest road you can take off the county road and drive onto the Randal property. It's past their driveway. Do you think that's how the person who took out the SD card got there or found the camera?"

"Could be. But why look at it then try to crush it under his foot?" Ryan folded up the map.

"Because there was something on it that either

made him mad or he didn't want anyone else to see." Shandra thought a moment. "Maybe the person I saw was J.W. He could have checked the card, saw something he didn't like, and ground it into the dirt."

"We'll know tomorrow when we find the card." Ryan leaned back, pulled Shandra down beside him with one arm draped over her shoulders, and promptly fell asleep.

Shandra remained snuggled against him until the call of nature forced her to get up. After using the bathroom, she placed a blanket over Ryan and closed herself into her bedroom. If he woke, he knew where the guest room was. He'd used it during his last murder investigation in Huckleberry.

Tomorrow they'd find the SD card. She donned her pajamas and crawled into bed. Sheba laid down at the end of the bed and was soon snoring. Shandra drifted into a state between sleep and awake. She heard Sheba snoring and Ryan tiptoeing past her door to the guest room, but Ella also hovered in her mind. Ella dangling the blue, crystal pendant.

Chapter Eighteen

The following morning Shandra woke with exuberance. They would find the SD card today and perhaps even the killer. And it was a good thing. They were only three days away from Conor's wedding to Ryan's ex-girlfriend. Shandra shook her head as she dressed. She had to quit thinking of the bride as Ryan's ex. She had a name. Lissa. But even thinking the name, it hissed in her head. The woman had to be blind to not see what kind of a catch Ryan would make.

Clanging in the kitchen hurried her morning routine. She walked into the room and found Ryan breaking eggs into a bowl.

"Morning," he said, adding milk to the mixture.

"What are you whipping up?" Shandra asked, stopping beside him and pouring a cup of coffee.

He kissed her temple. "French toast. I haven't had it in a while and you had all the ingredients."

"There aren't that many. Do you keep your place

stocked that poorly?" She leaned her backside against the counter next to Ryan and watched him cook.

"I'm not home a lot and when I am I tend to forget to buy groceries." He dipped bread in the egg mixture and placed it on the sizzling griddle.

"Will you be able to get away this weekend for the wedding?" Even though she had cold feet about attending the wedding, she wanted to go for Ryan's sake. He needed to show people Lissa didn't meant anything to him anymore.

"Unless I discover the murderer and need to move quickly, the sheriff knows where I'll be this weekend." Ryan plopped the cooked bread onto a plate. "Want to set out plates?"

"It's the least I can do with you cooking my breakfast." She laid two placemats on the counter, added plates and utensils, and refilled the coffee cup on the counter next to Ryan.

They sat and ate.

"This is really good. What did you put in here besides nutmeg?" Shandra asked after eating a piece and putting another on her plate.

"A bit of almond extract. I was happy to see you had some." Ryan took a drink of coffee.

"The two flavors work well together." Shandra finished the bread on her plate and placed her dishes in the sink. She faced Ryan. "Are we riding horses or driving and then on foot?"

"We'll take my rig. This excursion is part of the investigation. Mrs. Randal or Hasting can't throw us off the property." Ryan stood and deposited his dishes in the sink. "I'll warm up the Tahoe."

Shandra swung a dish rag at him. "Just because

you cooked you think you don't have to clean up the mess?"

"Exactly." He laughed, ducked, and disappeared out the back door with Sheba on his heels.

"Even my dog left me to clean up the mess." Shandra chuckled and cleaned up the dishes and kitchen. There wasn't much to clean up. Ryan was a clean cook.

She grabbed her coat, scarf, stocking cap, and mittens. Frost covered the ground this morning, proving summer was slowly giving way to fall.

Ryan sat in his car talking on the phone. Sheba sat by the driver's-side door peering up at the detective.

"Sheba, stay girl. You can visit Lil." Shandra waved to the barn and the big dog bounded across the space from the vehicle to the barn and disappeared around the side.

Shandra opened the door and sat in the passenger seat.

"I won't miss the rehearsal. Yes. You won't let me forget I'm the best man. Conor, I have to go." Ryan rolled his eyes then his face went stone still. "We'll need two rooms. Yes, I'll pay for both of them. I have to go." He punched the button on his phone and slid it into the holder on his belt.

"What was that about two rooms?" Shandra had a feeling she knew but wanted it confirmed.

"I have to be at the rehearsal dinner in Coeur d'Alene on Saturday night. It's ridiculous for us to drive back here afterward and turn around and go back the next morning." Ryan put the vehicle in reverse and held his attention on the side mirrors as he backed up.

"That's true, it is smarter and safer to stay in Coeur d'Alene. But you don't have to pay for my room. I'll take care of it myself." She was glad he told his brother they'd be in separate rooms. They hadn't known each other long enough or well enough to sleep together. She wasn't like a lot of her classmates in college who slept with every male they went on a date with. She had to like the guy enough to want to be that intimate. There had only been two men she'd slept with and both had burned her.

"Your call. I just felt since you were going to the wedding as a favor to me, the least I could do was pay for your room." Ryan headed the Tahoe down her lane.

"I'll pay. I plan on talking to a couple galleries Sunday morning. I can write it off as a business expense." She wanted to settle back in the seat but her mind and nerves buzzed just like when she came up with a new idea for a vase. They were going to find the SD card and it would reveal something the killer didn't want known. She was sure of it.

"Don't you want to get all gussied up for the wedding?" Ryan thought all women wanted to get their hair done and feel pampered on a wedding day.

"I'm not part of the wedding party. I've no need to be tortured. Everyone will be looking at the bride and her attendants. I'll just sit in the sidelines."

He had a feeling even if she wasn't getting all dolled up, she would still catch attention.

Ryan turned onto the county road. They passed the Randal driveway. The wrought iron gate was closed.

A mile down the road, Shandra shifted in her seat. "There. See that road. That has to be the one on the map."

He felt her anticipation. The energy she gave off started his adrenaline pumping. They could find the murderer or the identity of the murderer if they found the SD card. They crept up the old logging road avoiding pot holes and downed limbs. The vehicle swayed back and forth and rocked up and down as they travelled farther up the side of the mountain.

Time wise it felt as if they'd driven miles, but the end of the road arrived after a mile and a half.

Shandra bolted out of the vehicle the moment the engine died. "Did you think the map showed the spot almost directly above this road?"

Ryan smiled at her excitement. "Yes." He pulled out a global-positioning device. "I have the coordinates in here." He punched the button and started in the direction the device told him to go.

"Clever. Are the coordinates from the person who installed the cameras?" Her voice came directly behind him.

"Yes. He gave me all the information about the cameras." Ryan noted the distance between them and the location. "We have about a half-mile hike."

"Do you think I can't make it?" she chided.

"No. Just letting you know it's not around the next tree."

They continued up the mountainside for twenty minutes before the device said they were in the area.

Ryan stopped. "It was around here." He waved his hands out around him.

Shandra closed her eyes.

He waited, wondering if she was talking to her grandmother or just acclimating herself.

Her eyes opened and studied the area around them. She stared up at the tall pine and lodge pole. Walking around, her face pointed skyward, she stopped beside a tall pine and dropped to her knees.

"Here. It's here." She stirred the ground with her hands, raking her fingers back and forth in a two-foot circle.

"How do you know that is the spot?" Ryan dropped to the ground and dug in the area she had cleared.

"In my dream, I looked up at this tree. The light shone down on this spot."

Ryan couldn't deny she had been right before, but he was skeptical that in all this forest she could find the exact spot from a dream. Then his finger touched something flat with hard, round corners. He scraped some more and there in the dirt, label side up, was an SD card.

"I have it." He brushed the dirt off the card and held it up.

Shandra sat back on her haunches, smiling. "That will help you solve the murder."

"I hope it does." He turned it over in his hands. "There's some damage. I'll take it to the forensic lab right away." Ryan held out a hand. "Come on. We both have work to do." He helped Shandra stand and gave her a quick kiss on the cheek. "I don't understand your dreams, but they are helping me solve crimes."

"I don't understand them either, but I'm beginning to believe in them."

Ryan bagged and tagged the SD card and put it in a pocket of his backpack.

He led the way down the mountain, stopping now and then to discuss a plant or rock. The outing had turned into a nature walk by the time they returned to the Tahoe.

"I'll drop you off at your place and head for Coeur d'Alene." Ryan sat in the driver's seat and started the engine.

"You can drop me off at the end of my driveway. I'd like to continue walking. I've had inspirations for a new piece of art."

"As you wish." Ryan navigated the rough logging road and dropped Shandra at her driveway. "I'll call you when I find out anything."

"You better. I'm vested in this. Not only did I find the body, but I'm having dreams about it." Shandra exited the vehicle. "In case I don't hear from you beforehand, what time are you picking me up Saturday?"

"Rehearsal is at five-thirty with dinner afterward." Ryan wanted to say he'd pick her up at eight and spend the whole day with her, but he didn't want her thinking he'd make her hang out with his family that much. "How about one? We'll get there in time to settle into our rooms. I can make the rehearsal and then pick you up for the dinner."

"I'll be ready." She closed the door and headed up the driveway.

Ryan watched her walk the first fifty feet while calling the Sheriff's office. It astonished him how she had such little faith in her dreams when they had proven correct every time she had one. Perhaps she'd have a dream about them that would help her lower her guard.

"Weippe County Sheriff's Department, Officer Wyland speaking."

Ryan was relieved to hear Charles' voice. He wouldn't have to dodge personal questions from his good-intentioned sister.

"Charles, this is Detective Greer. I'm taking evidence relevant to the murder investigation in Huckleberry to Coeur d'Alene."

"I'll tell the sheriff and let others on the case know." Charles was all business.

"Thanks." Ryan hung up the call and pulled back onto the county road. He shoved the accelerator down. The sooner they discovered what was on the SD card, the better. If he could close this case by early Saturday morning, he could more thoroughly enjoy Conor's wedding and his date.

Chapter Nineteen

Shandra strolled up the driveway, conjuring up the forest plants she and Ryan had stopped to discuss. The coming of fall didn't create the same abundance of color that was found in spring and summer. The dull browns, tans, and fading greens weren't usually something that captured her attention. She was partial to bright colors. Loved when the leaves turned bright shades of red, yellow, and orange. But seeing the plants through Ryan's eyes had opened her to an idea for a vase.

Back at her studio, she immediately sat down and started molding clay and spinning it on her wheel. While her mind whirled with the drab tones she planned to use on the vase, flashes of brilliant blue, like the pendant she'd found, kept bursting into her mind.

"Why is the pendant on my mind?"

The door opened, allowing cold air to whisk around her. "Brrr. I think our Indian summer is about gone," she said.

Lil stood inside the door. "Yep. It's going to get cold tonight. I have the animals all set up in the barn."

Sheba entered and collapsed in her usual spot under the cooling table.

Shandra looked up from her project and noted the darkness outside the window. She stood and stretched. "I didn't realize I'd been at this all day."

"I figured your trip this morning brought on an idea. You've been in here for hours." Lil started tidying up the studio.

Shandra glanced at her vase. Another couple hours and it would be complete. She'd add the twig shaped handles tomorrow. Picking up a clean sheet, she settled the cloth over the vase. "I'll finish this in the morning."

"Good idea. I'll clean up in here, you go get something to eat." Lil shushed her out of the studio.

Sheba woofed and jogged out the door before Lil shut it.

"I think she just threw me out," Shandra said as she patted Sheba's head. "Come on. Let's get some dinner."

~*~

Ryan stood in the technology lab watching a forensic specialist clean up the SD card.

"You're lucky, this small crack doesn't appear to have damaged the data. If it had stayed in the ground through a rain storm more dirt would have compromised the data." The specialist glanced up. "You know I can send you the photos when I get them downloaded."

"I know. But I'm here and you said it would only take an hour. I'll wait." Ryan leaned against the wall, proving he had nowhere else to be.

"Suit yourself." The specialist went back to cleaning the card.

Ryan's phone buzzed. He glanced at the number and groaned. His little sister who lived in Coeur d'Alene. He stepped out of the lab and stood in the hallway.

"Hey Bridget, what's up?"

"I heard you're here, in town. Come by for dinner." Her tone was too sweet. She had to be up to something.

"I really should get back to Huckleberry. I'm in the middle of a murder investigation." She had to have found out about his trip to Coeur d'Alene from their sister Cathleen. She must have come on duty and saw the log book showing his whereabouts.

"You rarely have dinner with us. The kids are beginning to think Uncle Ryan doesn't exist anymore."

Tossing guilt on him with the nieces and nephew always worked. He had a soft spot for the little rug rats. "I'm not sure when I'll get there. I'm waiting on evidence."

"I'll have a plate warming for you if you don't make it by six."

The phone went quiet. Something was up. Bridget never called and got off the phone in less than twenty minutes.

The lab door opened. The specialist working on the SD card poked his head out. "I've got it working."

Ryan hurried into the lab. The first six photos were of animals, then a man and either a teenaged girl or a young woman dressed like most high schoolers showed up in the next seven frames. Each frame had the girl in less and less clothing and the man's hands all over her.

From the photos he'd seen at the Randal house and the newspaper articles, the man was J.W. Randal. There was never a clear photo of the girl. Her face was always turned from the camera, as if J.W. didn't want her completely recognized. Because he knew the camera was there. What did he plan to do with the photos? Keep them? But the last photo…a blue, flower-shaped necklace hung down her bare back.

Blackmail.

The necklace had been placed for the camera to see for a reason.

But who?

"Send those photos to my phone." He rattled off the number. That necklace was found at the murder site. Could that girl have been the murderer? If so, she appeared to be a minor. What happened to make her shoot the man? It didn't look like she was forced to take off her clothes, but the photos only showed flashes of what could have been happening. There was a strong possibility J.W. may have been saying things that made her feel threatened.

"Send prints of those photos to me at the Huckleberry Police Station." He studied the photo. "The man is the mauled victim from Huckleberry. Have techs use his size to determine the height and weight of the female. And if possible the age. I need all the info I can get to find her."

"I'll send this photo to Duncan, it has the best view of their height ratio."

"Have him call me with his findings." Ryan glanced at his watch. Mid-afternoon. He could be back in Huckleberry working the case in a little over an hour. It was three hours until dinner at Bridget's. He'd swing by there, say hi to the kids, and leave.

They'd see him Saturday night and Sunday at the wedding.

~*~

Feeling restless, Shandra decided to sit outside and watch the stars. The cold air sent her back in to grab a wool blanket. She wrapped the bright-colored covering around her and settled on the patio swing. Sheba sat, then slowly lowered her body to the paving stones in front of the swing.

Ryan had yet to call. "Is it taking that long to clean the card and discover the information?" she asked Sheba, patting the dog's head.

A muffled ragtime tune emitted from her blanket. Shandra reached into the pocket of the sweatshirt she wore and pulled out her phone.

Ryan.

"Hello," she answered.

"Hi. Thought you'd want to know what the SD card showed." His voice while warm held a bit of uncertainty.

"I was wondering. Did it take a long time to clean up the disk?" She wanted to know what he saw but from his greeting she wasn't sure he knew anything.

"It didn't take the techs long to bring up the photos. There are animals. Raccoons, deer, coyote, elk. What wasn't expected were pictures of Randal fooling around with what the techs have determined is most likely a female, and a minor one at that."

"I'm not surprised given what we already know about the man and Cecily's experience with him."
She'd caught the word determined. "Why did they have

to determine she was a minor?"

"There is never a clear picture of her face. Randal knew where the camera was and kept the girl turned. All that was captured on the card was her back." Ryan blew out a breath. "She was wearing the blue necklace we found."

Shandra sat up. "You think the young woman killed him?"

"I'm not sure. The whole thing looks staged. The necklace was placed dangling down her back for whoever looked at the photos to see. It has a significance to…someone." Ryan's voice faded.

"You think he was setting up someone for blackmail?" From what she'd discovered of the man so far, she was pretty sure he was not above blackmail.

"That's what I'm thinking. He set the whole thing up to get the photos to blackmail someone. But I don't understand why he didn't get the card unless he didn't want the girl to see she'd been photographed. So, whoever found the camera, saw the photos, and ground them into the dirt. The person he planned to blackmail or someone else?"

"If the pendant has a significance, we should be able to track it down. Start with the jewelers in Huckleberry, then show it around town. Someone would know who wears it." Shandra wanted to help him but wasn't sure how he'd feel about her inviting herself to go along with him.

"That's the plan for tomorrow. Want to meet me for lunch at Ruthie's?"

The hopefulness in his voice made her smile.

"Yes. I started a piece after you left today. I can finish it up in the morning and meet you about noon."

"Good. I'll have you take a look at the photos. With your artist's eye you might see something the techs missed." A pause. "See you tomorrow."

"Night." Shandra pushed the off button and leaned her head back against the cushion. Ryan wanted her to look at the photos. *I hope I can find something that helps.*

Chapter Twenty

Shandra finished the vase and drove into Huckleberry. The piece had turned out better than she'd visualized in her mind. The lines evoked promise. She smiled. It was the easy comradery she felt with Ryan that had helped her transform the clay into an inviting piece. Once the drab fall colors were splashed with the bright blue it would show that out of the dark could come hope.

She arrived at Ruthie's before Ryan.

"Morning, Shandra. You meeting that fine detective of yours?" Ruthie asked, placing a glass of water in front of her.

A smile spread across her lips. "He's not my detective, but yes, I am meeting him."

Ruthie laughed. "You may not think he's yours but he thinks you're his."

Shandra was jolted by the comment. She'd been treated like a possession by Carl and wasn't about to go that route again. "I'll have my usual."

Ruthie's smile disappeared. "Did I say something wrong?"

"No. You just jogged a memory." Shandra took a sip of water. A bad memory.

"Morning Detective," Ruthie called out as the door jingled.

Shandra glanced over her glass. Ryan smiled and strode forward. He might be pushy, tough, and persistent with people on his job, but he'd given her all the space she needed. He was nothing like Dr. Landers. She smiled. "There's my lunch date." Shandra waved a hand at the seat across from her.

Ryan laughed and placed his ball cap on the bench seat beside him. "It's a working lunch date for me."

Ruthie appeared at the end of the table. "What can I get you?"

"Iced tea, burger, and fries." Ryan smiled at Ruthie.

"They'll be out in ten." Ruthie pivoted and headed for the kitchen.

"Any luck with the jewelry stores?" Shandra asked.

He shook his head. "No. Everyone says it looks vintage but they didn't sell, repair, or clean it."

"If it's vintage that could mean it's a family heirloom." Shandra tapped her finger against her glass of water, thinking. "There's a chance it could be looked up on a vintage jewelry site. We wouldn't know who owns it, but we can narrow down when and where it was made and sold. That might help discover possibilities of who could own it."

Ryan held his phone out to her. "You didn't get a chance to look it over very closely the other day before I bagged it as evidence. Here's what it looks like in the photo."

Shandra made the photo larger and studied the jewelry. One of the stones appeared brighter. "There has to be a jeweler who knows this piece. It looks like one of the stones has been replaced." She glanced up at Ryan. "Can I see the pendant?"

"It's being held in the evidence room at the Huckleberry Police Station. We can go there after lunch. No one in Huckleberry repaired it." Ryan ran a hand across the back of his neck. "How did the piece you were working on turn out?"

She smiled, pleased he'd asked. "It's going to be one of my best pieces. You inspired it."

His eyes lit up and a smile spread across his chiseled features. "I did. How?"

"Our walk in the forest yesterday triggered an idea." She glanced down at the photo of the blue pendant. The pendant had a large part in the outcome of the vase as well.

"Did you try Hafersville or Missoula?" She handed his phone back. "Those are the other two close towns that would have jewelers. Or even Coeur d'Alene. It's not that far of a drive. Especially if they were already there and that's when they lost the stone."

Ryan leaned back as Ruthie placed their food in front of them.

"Enjoy."

The woman strolled away calling out to a customer walking through the door.

"I can check Hafersville and Missoula this afternoon. If nothing comes up, how do you feel about heading to Coeur d'Alene early tomorrow? We can canvas the jewelry stores and hit the art galleries before

I have to make an appearance at the rehearsal.”

“Only if you take me with you this afternoon. If you go on to Missoula, I’d like you to drop me off at the retirement center. I’ve been meaning to get over there and see Phil Seeton.” Shandra bit a sweet potato fry and studied Ryan. He knew Phil was her connection to her father and she was interested in how he died. He also wasn’t keen on her investigating her father’s death.

“If all you do is reminisce about your father and not try to build a conspiracy, I’d love to have you ride along this afternoon.”

Ryan watched Shandra. His words fell on deaf ears. She would talk to Seeton about whatever she wanted. He just hoped if she did come up with her father’s death being foul play, she’d come to him with the information she gathered and not confront the murderer.

“I can’t promise you we won’t talk about the day Daddy died.” The solemnness to her voice proved how much she’d cared for her father even as a four-year-old.

“I know you’d never keep the promise anyway.” Ryan reached across the table, placing his hand over hers. “Just promise if you discover your father’s accident wasn’t an accident, you talk it over with me before saying anything to anyone else.”

Her golden eyes peered into his. “That I can promise.”

He squeezed her hand. “Good. Eat.”

Ryan chatted about his visit with Bridget the day before while they ate. “I don’t know why my family is so curious about you. You’d think I hadn’t dated since Lissa.”

Shandra stopped in the act of biting her burger and

stared at him. "Have you dated since Lissa?"

He shrugged. "I had some dates in Chicago. But with my job it was hard to make plans in advance and know I'd keep them." His good mood soured thinking about Chicago and his undercover assignment. The one that had nearly killed him.

This time Shandra reached out to him. "I can tell something happened to you in Chicago. Something you don't want to talk about. When you're ready, I'll listen and not be judgmental."

She was too intuitive. He'd known that from the first time they'd met. But he'd done things to fit into the gang that a sane person wouldn't do. He'd thought cracking down on the violence the gangs had unleashed on the poorer neighborhoods would get him a promotion. Instead, it got him a near death wake-up call.

"When I feel the need to bare my soul, you're the one I'd feel the most comfortable telling." He turned his hand, clasping her palm in his.

Her eyes widened, before her lashes fluttered down, hiding her emotions behind a veil of dark lashes.

"You two need any refills?" Ruthie asked, her face beaming as her gaze leapt from him, to their clasped hands, to Shandra, and back to him.

"We're good." Ryan released Shandra's hand and tossed his napkin on his plate. "Ready to roll?"

"Yes." Shandra shoved her plate to the middle of the table and stood, pulling on her coat.

At the police station, Ryan signed the necklace out of the evidence room then left Shandra in the break room studying the blue flower with Hazel watching over the evidence. He printed out a copy of the photo from the email forensics sent him. If they couldn't connect the jewelry with someone, they were at a standstill. He did get a court order to look into the financial records of Vivian Randal, Cecily Wagner, the Hastings, Takagi, Smith, and because of the man's evasiveness when they'd talked about the photo, Clower. Cathleen and a deputy were pulling the financial records. He'd get a copy of those this evening when he returned from his road trip with Shandra.

He walked into the break room and found Shandra and Hazel visiting. The necklace sat on the table between them.

"Tell me you've seen this necklace before," Ryan said as he picked it up.

Hazel shook her head. "Sorry. It's pretty and I would have noticed it if I'd ever seen it."

"It definitely has had a jewel replaced." Shandra plucked the jewelry from his hand and pointed to a stone on the end of a petal. "It's this one. See how it's clearer, not as scratched as the rest." She turned the flower. "And this prong here…It's been patched."

Ryan held out his hand. Shandra dropped the necklace in his palm. He placed the jewelry in the evidence bag. "I'll return it to evidence and we better get on the road."

Ryan put the necklace in the evidence room and escorted Shandra out to his Tahoe.

~*~

Shandra was secretly happy they hadn't found a jeweler in Hafersville that had replaced the blue crystal. She'd get her visit with Phil.

On the drive to Missoula, Ryan restated his worry

over her digging up information about her father's death. But now that she was pushing forward trying to learn the truth, she felt it in her heart that his death wasn't an accident.

Ryan pulled into the retirement home.

She stepped out of the vehicle. "You'll know where to find me when you're finished."

"If he falls asleep and you want to leave give me a call," Ryan said.

"You think he'll fall asleep when he has a visitor?"

"He is an old man."

Shandra closed the door and waved him off. Now that she stood on the sidewalk in front of the retirement home, she was unsure of herself and her questions. Phil had been pretty persuasive the last time she was here that Daddy had been murdered. She'd tried to find out more information on the accident that killed Daddy, but she'd come up against some walls. Namely some of the officials involved in the rodeo that day were gone or mentally incapacitated.

She drew in a deep breath and walked through the doors.

The receptionist smiled. "May I help you?"

"I'm here to see Phil Seeton," Shandra said, walking up to the desk.

"Oh, he needs a visitor. He's not doing too well." The receptionist stood. "Sign in here."

Shandra signed in and followed the young woman down the hall to the room she'd visited while proving Lil was innocent of killing her lover.

The receptionist knocked on the door. "Mr. Seeton? You have a visitor." She eased the door open and then nodded. "He's awake."

"Thank you." Shandra entered the room. "Hi Mr. Seeton. Do you remember me? Shandra Higheagle."

The thin man in a sweatshirt, jeans, big silver buckle and cowboy boots looked up from the magazine he was reading. He smiled, revealing a mouth without teeth in his narrow, sallow face. He yanked the reading glasses from his long nose and waved the magazine at a chair by the desk.

"I sure do remember you. How you doing, girl?"

Shandra pulled the chair closer to his, sat, and grasped his extended hand. "I'm doing well." She glanced at the magazine. *American Cowboy.* "I see you're still keeping up on things."

"Once a rodeo cowboy, always a rodeo cowboy. You going to the National Finals?" His face lit up saying National Finals.

"No. I've not been a fan of rodeo knowing how Daddy died." It was the truth. She'd shied away from anything to do with rodeo. Her mom didn't care one way or the other. Adam, her step-father, had been adamant she didn't need to get caught up in the life. Even though he still raised rodeo rough stock.

"It's something in the blood. Your daddy sure had it. He loved to ride the horses no one else could ride." Phil's eyes dimmed as he reminisced.

"I've studied the events enough to know riders didn't choose their rides, they were drawn. How did they draw the horses back then?" Shandra released Phil's hand.

He settled back in his chair. "The names of the horses went in one cowboy hat and the names of the cowboys went in the other. The names were drawn one out of the horses, one the cowboys, and then matched together."

"Who was present during this process?" If she could figure out if Daddy riding that horse was a fluke she'd be satisfied, but her gut told her he'd been matched with a horse known to stomp the riders when they hit the ground for a reason.

"Back then the secretary of that rodeo drew the names while the stock contractor and a judge or association official watched." Phil went thoughtful for a minute or so. "Can't say for sure, but I think Adam Malcolm's family provided the stock for that rodeo."

Shandra nodded. She'd looked up information on the rodeo Daddy participated in that last time and it was indeed stocked by the Malcolm family. From the comments Phil had made the first time she'd visited him, she had an inkling there was a reason her step-father didn't want her digging up the death of her father.

A soft knock accompanied by the receptionist's voice interrupted their conversation.

Chapter Twenty-one

"Mr. Seeton. You have another visitor."

Ryan strolled into the room. "Good to see you again, Mr. Seeton." Ryan stepped forward and shook hands.

"You still hanging out with this cop?" Phil asked with a twinkle in his eye.

"Yes. He was my ride this way, so be nice to him." Shandra stood. "Thank you for all your information."

"You're welcome, any time." Tears glistened in the old man's eyes.

Shandra bent down and kissed his cheek. "Don't worry. I'll be back."

"I'll hold you to that."

"We have a two-hour drive back and an early start in the morning," Ryan said, holding the door open.

"I know." She smiled at Phil. "See you soon."

Out in the parking lot, Shandra took a long, deep breath. Not only to clear her lungs of the antiseptic air in the retirement home, but to clear her mind of the thoughts that had ricocheted around in her head as she and Phil talked.

"You okay?" Ryan stood beside her unlocking her door on the SUV.

"Yes. Just sorting through what Phil told me." Her hair caught in the wind and blew across her face. She shove it to the side and climbed into the vehicle. Having her hand fall short of the ends since Tammy took too much off only intensified her vow to never go near a hair salon again.

Once Ryan was in the driver's seat and starting the car, she asked, "The talk about an early start, you didn't find a jeweler who worked on the pendant."

"Not a jeweler in this town has seen the necklace." He drove out of the parking lot. "Want to get dinner here before heading back to Huckleberry?"

"My burger has worn off." She smiled at Ryan. He was so thoughtful. "We're going to get back to Huckleberry late. Do you want to stay at my place tonight? That way you don't have to drive the extra distance to town tonight and back in the morning."

He glanced at her and smiled. "That would give me more sleep. If you don't mind."

"I wouldn't have asked if I minded." She studied him as he navigated through the Missoula traffic. "You know, as much as you've been staying at my place you might want to leave some clothes there."

His head pivoted, and he stared at her. "You know, as much as I stay over already people are talking."

She put a hand on his arm. "I don't mind having my name linked with yours. Besides having a cop sleeping in my house is the best kind of security."

"I'll only stay with you when I have cases in this area that prevent me from working out of the sheriff's department."

"I know. That's all I want. For now." She stared out the window wondering at her offer. She was fond of Ryan. And she knew he wouldn't pressure her to go beyond her comfort level. This day and age she didn't care what the community thought of her. They were good friends.

The vehicle slowed and Ryan pulled into a restaurant parking lot. He leaned her direction, opened the glove box, and put his gun and badge inside. He locked the compartment and kissed her. "I'm hungry."

She peered into his eyes. The gleam in them made her wonder if he was talking about food. The thought warmed and scared her. She couldn't think of a commitment to anyone until she'd come to grips with her own bad choice in men and her father's death.

Shandra couldn't shake the information Phil told her. She had an even stronger feeling her father's death wasn't an accident.

The door on her side opened. Ryan leaned against the door. "You want to tell me what Phil said that has you in another world right now?"

She shook her head, clearing the thoughts away. "Maybe later. I still need to digest some of the information."

Ryan knew she was stalling. Something about Shandra's meeting with the Seeton guy had her deep in thought. It was more than digesting the information. He escorted her into the restaurant.

If she remained this distracted all weekend, they

weren't going to have a very good time at the wedding.

She studied the menu and he studied her. The guarded aura she'd exuded the first time they met had returned.

The waitress left with their orders. Ryan picked up his iced tea, took a sip, and cleared his throat. "Are you going to be this distracted all weekend?"

Shandra's forehead wrinkled in a frown. "No. Once I sleep on the information it won't bother me." She picked up her cup of tea and sipped.

"I don't know. You're even more thoughtful than the last time you visited Seeton." Ryan needed to know what they said in order to make sure she came to no harm.

"Forget about my visit. You have a case to solve." Shandra set her cup down. "So far, no jewelry store in the immediate area worked on that pendant. Maybe it is someone who moved to the area recently."

"I thought of that and had Blane pull all the names of people who moved to Huckleberry in the last year." The results confirmed his thoughts. "The only people who permanently moved here recently are male. Not a lot of people move to Huckleberry. Most of the transient labor in the winter time are only here for six months."

"You have no way to find out who the woman is?" Shandra took another sip of tea.

"The techs at forensics place her in her late teens, about five-foot-eight judging from her difference in height to Randal and about a hundred-and-twenty pounds." A thought came to him.

"How tall are you?" She had to be about the same height as the girl.

"Five-nine. Why?"

"What size shoe do you wear?" Ryan had a feeling he knew who the other boot print belonged to.

"Why, are you planning to buy me a new pair of boots? I happen to have my eye on the Sidewinder by Dan Post." She smiled sweetly.

"That's a thought, but no. There were two pairs of boot tracks besides Randal's at the murder site. One was either a small men's or a women's track."

"I wear a size eight in boots." She waited until the waitress cleared the plates then leaned closer. "Do you think the girl lured him out there and someone else shot him?"

"I'm not sure about anything except the three sets of boot tracks and the necklace." He drank the last of his tea. "Do you want dessert?"

"No. I'd rather get home. I can treat you to either ice cream or brownies I keep in the freezer for guests." She stood, sliding her arms into the sleeves of her coat.

"If I get you home quickly, can I have both?" He was a sucker for home-baked goods.

Shandra laughed. "No hurry. You can have both."

The drive back to Shandra's ranch was uneventful and quiet. Ryan liked that they could sit in silence without it feeling awkward. He thought back to when he'd dated Lissa. She had to have conversation every minute. It was exhausting. At first he found it funny and laughed it off as part of what he liked about her. Later he found it annoying. When did I figure out we weren't an ideal match? When he was overseas in the military. Hearing the other soldiers talk about their significant others, he'd realized he didn't get as animated or excited to receive her letters. Not like he did to hear from his mom and sisters.

"What are you thinking on so hard over there?" Shandra's voice asked in the darkness filling the vehicle.

"How I'm glad Conor and Lissa are getting married. I would have made a lousy husband to her." That he was sure of.

"Why do you say that?" She shifted in the seat as much as the seat belt would allow.

He glanced over, catching a glimpse of her face from the lights of a passing car.

"I'm not the type to settle into a safe career. She's insecure and needs the security of a husband twenty-four seven."

"But your job is protecting people. She should understand that would take you away."

Shandra's comment warmed him. She understood his job. "She never understood my desire to join the military. When I got back, we were pretty much over. When I told her I was headed to a job as a policeman in Chicago, she told me to do whatever I wanted, we were through."

"That's cold!" Anger vibrated in Shandra's voice.

He laughed. "Cold but the best thing that could have happened. She and I would have made each other miserable. I'm sure of it now."

"Then you are going to the wedding tomorrow without any regrets?" She settled back against the seat, facing forward.

"Yes. The only regret is that we didn't end it before I went overseas. Getting her short, cold letters when everyone else talked non-stop about their girlfriends and wives waiting for them hurt."

Her hand rested on his arm. "We can't change the past. Only use it to move forward."

"I agree. And I'm grateful to you for being my guest at the wedding festivities over the weekend." He placed his hand on top of hers and squeezed.

"I wouldn't miss it. I have to see these sisters who give you fits." She laughed as he pulled into her driveway.

"That's my only fear."

They laughed all the way up her bumpy drive.

The lights shone bright outside and inside the house.

"Wow, things are lit up." He stopped the SUV and turned off the engine.

"Lil always turns the lights on when I'm coming home after dark. It's such a nice welcome to see the house lit up." Shandra slipped out of the vehicle and walked up the scattered pavers to the front porch.

A large dark object charged around the side of the studio.

Before Ryan could react, a wide, wet tongue licked his face as two big paws landed on his shoulders.

"Sheba you big goof. What are you doing licking me? You're a guard dog. The least you could do is growl." Ryan ruffled the big mutt's ears.

She returned to all four legs and trotted into the house behind Shandra.

Ryan shook his head and retrieved a bag of extra clothes and toiletries he kept in the rig for overnight assignments.

Tomorrow they'd drive through the county seat,

and he'd collect the clothes he needed for the weekend and his gift to the newlyweds—a vase by Shandra he'd purchased at the summer art event he had attended to gather information for the first murder he and Shandra solved together.

"You coming in? The cold wind is howling through here." Shandra had taken her coat off and held a steaming mug in each hand.

"Coming." He hustled through the door and closed it tight behind him.

"Where were your thoughts out there?" She asked, handing him a frothy cup of hot chocolate after he placed his bag in the guest room.

"I was thinking about how we met."

She laughed, the husky laugh that had caught his attention several months ago. "Me in handcuffs and you sternly studying me."

He laughed. "You have to admit, Blane was doing what he was supposed to do."

"Except he lacked a crucial skill…listening." She laughed and curled her legs under her on the couch.

Ryan settled on the other end. Glancing down, he noticed a very good likeness of the necklace they'd found in the forest. "What's this?" He picked up the sketch colored with pencil.

"I can't get the pendant out of my head. Even today when I was working on the vase it kept swirling into my thoughts. I think I'm going to incorporate the blue color into the colors of the newest vase."

"This is nearly a dead ringer for the flower." He studied it some more. "You did this from memory?"

"That and it was in a dream I had." Her chin dipped, and her eyes stared into her hot chocolate.

"This may seem silly but after a dream where Ella has shown herself, if I close my eyes, I can see the images of the dream clearly. That's what I did in the forest yesterday. Closed my eyes and saw the whole scene." She stared into his eyes. "Even the man's back. He wore a light-weight jacket. Black. His pants were a dark green." She closed her eyes. "He had on a stocking cap, hiding the color of his hair. The hat was black."

Her lashes lifted. Pale golden eyes peered into his. "I would know this man from the back if I saw him."

He didn't doubt she would. "Maybe tomorrow morning we'll have a suspect or two."

Shandra rose from the couch. "I'll get that brownie and ice cream I promised you."

Ryan watched her pad out of the room on bare feet, Sheba walking behind flailing her fluffy black tail in the air.

He stared at the replica of the necklace. If they discovered the owner tomorrow while canvassing the jewelers in Coeur d'Alene, he could have a suspect in custody by Monday.

Chapter Twenty-two

Shandra walked into a jewelry store in front of Ryan. They'd started with a list of seven stores and three specialty jewelers. They'd hit all the specialty jewelers and had only three more on the list to visit.

"How may I help you?" The older woman glanced at their hands and smiled. "An engagement ring perhaps?"

"No, we're not—" Ryan stumbled. He flashed his badge. "I'm with the Weippe County Sheriff. We are trying to locate the owner of this piece of jewelry. We believe it has been repaired recently." He held out the photo of the pendant.

Shandra sidled up beside Ryan. It was fun watching him squirm. Nearly every store they'd entered the employees had insinuated the same remark as this woman blurted out.

"Yes. I remember we worked on this last year. Not worth a lot but it had sentimental value to the family." She glanced up. "You sure I couldn't interest you in an engagement ring?"

"No. But I'd like the name of the family who brought this in." Ryan tapped the photo.

"Browse. I'll look through my records." She winked at Shandra. "Over there are the engagement rings."

Shandra couldn't stop the giggle tickling her throat.

"Care to browse the engagement rings?" Ryan asked, waving to the case the woman had indicated.

"No, thank you. I like my single status right now." She wandered instead over to a case with a set of silver bangle bracelets.

The woman returned with a slip of paper. "This is the family."

Ryan glanced at the paper. His gaze leveled on the woman. "You're positive?"

"Yes. I even have photos of the pendant missing the stone and the one we set." The woman watched him. "Is there something wrong?"

"No. Nothing."

Shandra could tell the name he was given puzzled Ryan. "Could I look at these please?" She pointed to the set of bangles shining in the fake lighting.

The woman grinned and hurried behind the glass case. She pulled out the bracelets.

They slid nicely over Shandra's hand and clanked as she moved her hand around. "I'll take these." She took the price tag off and paid the woman.

Standing out on the street, she tapped Ryan's arm. "Who does the pendant belong to?"

"Donna Clower."

"A relation to the Fish and Game officer?" Shandra didn't like the way her thoughts were heading. "Is that a daughter?"

"No, that's Melvin Clower's wife. She wasn't the one wearing it in the photos." Ryan opened the passenger door of his Tahoe.

Shandra climbed in. The daughter was fooling around with J.W. When and how did the Fish and Game officer find out?

Ryan sat in the driver's seat. "I thought he acted strange when I fished the family photo out of the pile of files on his desk. And when I brought up the daughter he told me I was too old for her."

"He thought you were looking to date his daughter?" Shandra couldn't imagine anyone thinking Ryan would be interested in a teenaged girl.

"Yes. I explained I had a woman I was dating."

"Meaning me?" She raised an eyebrow. They were dating in a way. But she wasn't ready to say they were a couple.

He smiled. "Yeah, you. I don't spend my working and off time with anyone else."

She knew he didn't have time to date. A smile tipped her lips. He made time for her. She knew he wanted more than friendship and his allowing her time to get to know him and not compare him to her past failures wasn't lost on her.

"What are you going to do with the information we found?" She knew he had an obligation to turn over the information, but she also knew he felt he had a vested interest in bringing in J.W.'s murderer.

"I'm going to put this information in the file and enjoy the rest of the weekend. I don't believe anyone in the Clower family will go out and shoot anyone else this weekend. I'll deal with it on Monday." He put the vehicle in drive. "Where is the gallery you wanted to check out?"

Shandra gave him directions, and they spent the time until the rehearsal wandering through the galleries and talking with the owners. She was pleased to see Ryan had an eye for art and some insightful thoughts about each piece.

~*~

Ryan greeted his family with hugs and slaps on the back. He knew Lissa's family from the years they'd dated. He was greeted warmly by them and so was Shandra. Watching his mother and Cathleen lead Shandra away from the gazebo where the vows would be said, while he had to pay attention to the order of events for the wedding, had his attention pulled in two directions.

"Ryan, are you even paying attention?" Conor asked.

"Huh? Yeah. I stand here and hand you the ring when the preacher asks for it." Ryan was struck again at how calm Conor was for tying the knot tomorrow.

"I can see why you're distracted. Your date is a looker." Conor's gaze traveled to the spot where Shandra and their mother and sister stood.

"Hey, you stole my first girlfriend, keep your grubby hands and eyes off this one." Ryan said it jokingly, but he meant every word.

"I'm completely in love with Lissa. I don't want your woman. I'm just admiring and saying you have a good eye." Conor put a hand on his shoulder. "Here comes Lissa, at least look like your mind is on doing a good job."

This was his first look at Lissa since they broke up six years ago. He felt nothing. He'd dreaded this moment, half afraid all the feelings and hurt he'd harbored for so long would rush out and strangle him. Watching her walk toward him, he felt nothing other than gratitude that she made his big brother so happy.

Ryan moved his gaze past the woman approaching and studied the three huddled under a tree. What was his mom and sister telling Shandra? Because from what he could see they were doing all the talking.

A slap on the back tore his gaze from under the tree where the women stood.

"Pay attention." Conor glared at him and turned his gaze on his soon-to-be wife.

The preacher walked them through the ceremony, the bride and groom walked down the area marked off as the aisle. Ryan moved to the middle and stuck out his elbow to escort the maid of honor, Lissa's sister, down the makeshift aisle behind the happy couple.

His mom and sister had moved on to capture Conor and Lissa. At the line depicting the last row of chairs, Ryan released the maid of honor and strode over to Shandra.

"What were mom and Cathleen talking to you about?" he asked. His gut squiggled just like when he was a kid and thought someone had tattled on him.

"We were discussing some final touches to the decorations. They thought since I was an artist I might be a natural at decorating." She nodded toward the wedding entourage. "Shouldn't you be over there in case they have more instructions?"

"I know what to do. This isn't the first wedding I've been a best man at." He had fond thoughts of his friend Langston's wedding and not so fond thoughts of the wedding he'd attended as the best man while infiltrating the Cobra gang.

"Come on, it looks like everyone is getting ready to head to dinner." Ryan had to let his time in Chicago become a foggy memory. It was the only way he could get on with his life. He'd betrayed the gang. Something none of them would forget any time soon. His only consolation was the fact they would never learn his real name. The head of the gang task force had made sure even the cops who knew he was a mole didn't know his real name. He'd told the chief the only way he'd go undercover was with a different name and identity to keep his family safe.

Fingers snapped in front of his face. "Earth to Ryan. Where were you?" Shandra slid her arm around his. "You keep telling me this wedding doesn't bother you, but you've been wandering off in your mind a lot this weekend."

"Sorry. Lots of memories that aren't pleasant filter in." He smiled and vowed to only think of the present.

"Unpleasant memories of your family or the ex?"

While her intuitiveness intrigued him it wasn't pleasant to have it used on him. "Mostly the ex." He wasn't ready, and may never be ready, to tell her about Chicago.

"She seems pleasant the little I've seen of her." Shandra stopped when the rest of the group entered the dining room of the country club where the wedding was being held.

Ryan watched her study the room. A large table was set up close to the door. The wedding party were taking seats.

"What's the matter?" Ryan grasped her forearms, making her face him.

She sighed. "Your mother and sister didn't pry, but their comments definitely made me feel like they were trying to find out exactly how intimate we are." She stared into his eyes. "Please don't try to be overly affectionate or do things for me you wouldn't normally. We aren't teenagers or for that matter young lovers. Just treat me like you have been."

Ryan studied her. Some man in her past had hurt her. He'd already come to that conclusion, but he now realized she'd been used as an ornament or trophy by the man as well.

"You think because my brother is getting married I need to prove I have a woman too?"

She half nodded.

"I wouldn't want to endanger our friendship by being that kind of person." He linked their arms. "Come on. We're friends enjoying being part of the wedding party."

He escorted her to their seats at the table. Before his mom could do the introductions, he set the record straight. "Everyone, this is my friend Shandra Higheagle. Would you each tell her your name and your connection to the bride and groom."

Shandra gave him a brief grin and then concentrated on the other guests.

Ryan hadn't thought about checking out Shandra's past. The more he learned about her past relationships, he understood how badly a man had hurt her. He didn't think she'd put up with physical abuse, but she gave indications there had been some kind of hold over her.

Chapter Twenty-three

Sunday afternoon, Shandra sat at a table in front of the country club private dining room. She'd tried to squeeze out of getting special treatment, but the attendants' guests were each given a place at the head table. Ryan sat near the middle next to his brother with her sandwiched between Ryan and one of Conor's friends and groomsman, Sherman Johnson. It turned out he was half Palouse. His mother was from the tribe, his father Caucasian.

"The Greers have always had Indian friends but I never thought one would have an Indian girlfriend." Sherman had a way of talking that made her lean closer, hoping the words would come out a little bit louder and faster.

"I'm not his girlfriend. I'm his friend." This was the first time she'd had to defend her friend status. The men who hit on her before the meal disappeared the minute Ryan walked her direction.

"Sure, you aren't. That's why he's given every man who looks at you a glare." The man's slow dialogue dug in more than if he said the words with emphasis.

"He…" she really couldn't refute that claim. He had been acting like a jealous boyfriend. But it had also kept the other men a safe distance from her. Which is all she wanted. She wasn't here to make merry. She was supporting a friend.

"Ahhh, see you can't say different." Sherman leaned a little closer.

"Shandra, I have someone I want you to meet." Ryan pulled her chair back.

Thankful to get away from Sherman, she stood and grasped the hand Ryan extended to her. She knew holding hands would get the tongues wagging but it felt right to walk with him this way. Being by his side, holding his hand, having him kiss her. They had all become second nature and felt right. After Carl, she hadn't planned to get involved with another man, ever. But the man holding her hand and leading her toward his family's table was making her see a future that wasn't so lonely.

They stopped at the family table.

"Shandra, this is my father, Ephraim Greer."

The pride in Ryan's voice was unmistakable. The man had been missing from the festivities the night before. According to the family it had been a farm emergency.

A man the spitting image of Conor, only two decades older, stood and held out his hand. "I understand you met my son under interesting circumstances." He motioned for her to take the empty space next to him. "Take Colleen's seat, she's off greeting everyone."

Shandra sat. Ryan stood behind her.

"Yes, I was handcuffed and he'd thought I'd killed someone," she said, narrowing her gaze.

Ephraim laughed loudly and wiped tears from his eyes. He looked up at his son. "Boy, you're supposed to handcuff a beautiful lady after you have her consent."

Her face heated. Unsure how to react, she glanced up at Ryan. His red face and gaze darting around the table proved he was embarrassed too.

"Thanks Pop. Now Shandra won't want to come to family gatherings." Ryan reached down and grasped Shandra's hand. "We have to get going. I'm working a case and need to get back."

"It was nice meeting all of you," she said, making eye contact with all of Ryan's immediate family.

He led her over to his brother. "Conor, we need to go. I have a case I'm working on."

"You have to stay for the cake," Lissa said, standing beside Conor.

"We can't. Ryan needs to get back to his work and I need to get back to mine. Thank you for allowing me to tag along with Ryan." Shandra smiled at the bride and groom and followed Ryan to the door. "Don't you need to say goodbye to your mother?" she asked, glancing over her shoulder and catching a glimpse of Colleen pointing a finger at Ephraim.

"Nope. She'll call me and ask what Pop did to make me leave." There was humor in his voice.

She stopped just inside the country club doors. "You took me over to your father knowing he'd say something that would give you an excuse to leave." She slapped him on the chest with her pocketbook. "You'd rather make a scene than just slip out."

"This way my mom and sisters will all be sorry for Pop's behavior and not bug me about you for a while." He smiled. "Come on. I do have a case to solve."

He gave the valet the ticket for his pickup, a green Ford, and they were soon driving down Highway 90 back to Huckleberry.

"Are you going to confront the Clowers?" Shandra asked.

"I can't. Not until I have more evidence than they own the necklace."

"But the photos of the girl wearing the necklace. Isn't that enough proof?" Shandra couldn't shake the feeling they were missing something else.

"It proves nothing. We don't have a good photo of her face. It could be someone who stole or borrowed the necklace. The photos only prove she and Randal were fooling around, not that she murdered him."

"But the smaller footprints could be hers. She killed J.W. and told her father. He knew about the wildlife cameras. He went to the murder site and removed the camera that would prove his daughter killed J.W." Shandra liked her theory.

"Buy why did she kill him? I need to find a motive. There is more motive for Clower killing him. Especially if he's the one who found the first camera and ground the SD card into the dirt."

Shandra sighed and leaned back in the seat. "I see why you need more evidence. I would think you could confront Mr. Clower about his daughter and J.W. That might get you something to start with."

"I had Deputy Speaks write up a warrant for the

financials of all the people involved in this investigation. The skillful way the girl's face was kept from the camera but the necklace was showcased, makes me think blackmail was involved. The financial records should show us the victim and hopefully lead to the murderer."

Shandra studied Ryan. He liked his job. It showed in the way he was thorough in his investigations.

"Do you think it was someone other than Mr. Clower's daughter, but J.W. wanted to make it look like it was her?" Shandra didn't like the idea J.W. had gone to such tactics to get out of his illegal hunting allegations.

"It would make sense Randal would target Clower to get him to back off. But stupid. Too many people knew about the allegations. Clower couldn't back off." Ryan ran a hand across the back of his neck. "Let's talk about something else. I'll have to face all this when I get back to Huckleberry."

"It was a nice wedding," Shandra said. It was the type of wedding at one time she'd dreamed of. That was until she'd witnessed the dysfunctional marriage between her mother and step-father and discovered the true nature of the two males she'd loved. Or thought she'd loved. She sighed deeply. Love was highly overrated.

"Yeah. A bit tame from what Lissa had told me she wanted twelve years ago." He smiled. "I liked it. Just the right amount of ceremony but mostly family oriented."

Ryan pulled into Warner, the county seat of Weippe. The small house he rented was on the outskirts of town. Shandra had remained outside, placing her luggage into his pickup when they stopped on the trip to Coeur d'Alene. This time he needed to change, not just grab his bag.

He turned into his driveway. "Grab your bags. We'll toss them in the Tahoe and go inside. I need to change and repack my bag."

"How much longer do you think the Randal murder will keep you in Huckleberry?" Shandra asked.

"I hope it's cleared up in a couple more days. If I get good leads from the bank statements and can link Clower to Randal." Ryan parked, killed the engine, and faced Shandra. "Does your invitation to stay at your place still stand?"

She stared into his eyes. "Why wouldn't it?"

"You've met my family, saw how they are pushing us together. I don't want their zealousness to make you think I'm in a hurry to tie the knot." He'd witnessed Shandra retreat a little more each time someone called them a couple. Something in her past had her skittish of marriage.

"I didn't invite your family to stay with me, I invited you." She touched his cheek. "You've not asked and I'm not ready to tell anyone of my stupidity. It makes me feel naïve and vulnerable when I think about it. But one day, when I feel I really know you and can trust you completely, I'll tell you about my past with men."

Ryan held her hand, turned his head, and kissed her palm. "When you're ready to tell me, I'll be here to listen."

"Thank you." She cleared her throat and drew her hand into her lap. "What kind of a bachelor pad do you live in?" Shandra opened the door and slipped out.

Ryan smiled. She wasn't ready, but her actions gave him hope that she would eventually feel comfortable enough with him to take their relationship to the next step.

He hopped out of the cab and into the back of the pickup. Unlocking the truck box, he pulled out his duffel and Shandra's travel bag.

She reached up taking her bag and his duffel.

His phone beeped as he crawled out of the pickup. "Greer.

"The warrant came through. I sent the financials to you in an email. I think you'll find them interesting," Speaks said.

"Thanks. I'm changing here in Warner but will be back in Huckleberry in less than an hour."

"How was your brother's wedding?" Speaks asked. He'd met Conor at the sheriff's office when one of Conor's clients was arrested for drunk driving.

"Nice." Ryan continued climbing out of the pickup and unlocked the Tahoe. Shandra placed her bag in the vehicle and headed up his walkway.

"I gotta go. Thanks again for taking care of the paperwork." Ryan ended the call and followed Shandra to his front door. "Keep in mind this is a bachelor pad, but my mom comes by once a week and cleans."

Shandra laughed. "Your mother comes by and cleans your house? I thought you said she taught you to cook. Didn't she teach you to clean up after yourself?"

He shoved the door open and waved her in. "Yes, I know how to clean up after myself. But there are times when I'm not home long enough to take out the garbage, wash my sheets, or vacuum. And I pay her."

Shandra walked into the small living room and twirled. "I see what you mean about a bachelor pad. With your interest in art you'd think you'd have more than a velvet paint-by-number of dogs playing poker."

Ryan laughed. "In all fairness, that was here when I moved in. Like I said, I'm not here much. It's more of a place to keep my clothes and sleep." He continued through the living room to the bedroom. "Make yourself at home. I'll only be five-ten minutes."

"M-hhmm."

He glanced back and found Shandra on the couch flipping through his *Guns & Ammo* magazine.

Grinning, he continued to the bathroom, dumped the dirty clothes from his duffel into the clothes basket, slipped out of the monkey suit he wore for the wedding, and changed into his usual jeans, flannel shirt, cowboy boots, and shoulder holster. Back in the bedroom, he put clean clothes in the duffel, clipped his badge to his belt and slid his Glock into the shoulder holster.

Returning to the living room, he found Shandra still reading the magazine.

"Find a gun you like?" he asked, sitting on the couch beside her.

"I've never shot a hand gun. Growing up, I learned how to shoot rifles. Adam wouldn't let me ride alone in the spring unless I had a rifle with me. We had trouble with cougars getting into the cattle when they were calving." She tapped the page. "I like the look of this one."

Ryan peered down at the page. Her finger was on a revolver.

"A revolver is good." He thought it was a good

idea considering she and Lil lived alone on the mountain. "How do you plan to use it?"

"A rifle is bulky to carry when I ride. After finding J.W., I started thinking I should be armed while riding."

"I agree. I'll go grab a couple of my hand guns. You can shoot them and see what you like the best." Ryan stood.

"That's a good idea. I haven't a clue what would be a good one for me." She closed the magazine.

Ryan returned to his bedroom, opened the closet, and dialed the lock on the gun safe at the back of the closet. His safe held a huge selection. Several different hunting rifles, sniper rifles, and handguns. He selected two automatics and two revolvers, slid them into a carrying case, and closed the safe.

Back in the living room, he handed the case to Shandra to carry to the Tahoe. "We'll have shooting practice. When you decide what you like, I'll teach you how to clean it. Then I'll take you to a reputable gun seller and you can purchase your own."

"I know how to clean my rifles, but I imagine a hand gun is going to be a bit more complicated." She raised the case. "Thank you. I've been contemplating this a while. The last week kind of pushed me to make a decision."

Ryan stored his duffel and the gun case in the back seat. "There's nothing wrong with having a gun for protection. Especially if you know how to use it."

They both took their seats in the vehicle. On the drive to Huckleberry, Ryan described the differences in the guns he'd brought for her to try.

Darkness shrouded the side streets of Huckleberry

as they drove through the town.

"Over there. Isn't that Red Hasting?" Shandra said, pointing to a man stumbling along the sidewalk.

Chapter Twenty-four

Ryan had witnessed many drunks. This man didn't stumble like a drunk. He appeared disoriented as he grasped the street light in front of the donut shop.

"I'm going to check him out." He swung the car into the side street.

"Stay put," he said, exiting the vehicle.

The man was Hasting. He barely raised his head when Ryan approached. "Mr. Hasting can I help you?"

The man stared at him. His eyes jiggled back and forth. He sucked in air. "C-can't b-r-ea-th-he," he slurred.

Ryan put an arm around Red, holding him up, and headed to the vehicle.

Shandra hopped out, opened the back door, and shoved their bags to the far side of the back seat.

"I think he's drugged." Ryan lowered Hasting into the back seat, closed the door, and hopped in the driver's seat.

He drove to the Emergency Care Center next to the clinic. He jumped out and banged on the locked door before reading the notice next to the door. *After hours call: 777-2929.*

Punching in the numbers Dr. Porter's name came up. The phone rang twice.

"Hello?"

"Doc, I've got Red Hasting down here at the Emergency Center. He's having trouble breathing and looks bad."

"I'll be there in five minutes."

The phone went silent. Ryan turned from the building. Shandra had the back door open and was talking to Hasting.

Ryan reached them in four strides.

"Red. Red stay awake. Did you drink too much?" Shandra asked, opening the man's top two buttons on his shirt. The way he sucked air into his lungs she wanted to help him get as much as he could.

"N-no-t d-rrrr-u-n-k. O-nnn-e d-rrrr-i-n-k." He dug at the collar of his shirt even though she'd opened it. "C-a-nnn-t b-r-ea-the."

"Doc Porter's on his way," Ryan said from behind her. He moved to her side. "Hasting, where did you have your drink?"

"M-m-m-a-a-x-x-i-e—" He gasped, grasping his throat.

"He's not breathing!" Shandra cried, grabbing an arm and trying to pull him out of the vehicle and onto the sidewalk.

Ryan grabbed his other arm. Together they pulled him out. Ryan started quick chest compressions. Shandra held his head straight, hoping to keep his airways open.

A car squealed to a stop.

Dr. Porter rushed by her, unlocked the emergency doors, and disappeared. He came back with a box and respirator. He showed her how to use the respirator and then ripped Red's shirt open and applied a gel to the paddles.

"All Clear." He placed the paddles on Red's chest. The motionless body jerked.

Dr. Porter sat back on his heels. Red didn't move. The doctor zapped him again. His body jerked and went still.

Setting the paddles on the open defibrillator box, Dr. Porter checked for breathing and pulse. He glanced at his watch. "I proclaim this man dead at eight twenty-three p.m."

Shandra stared down at the man who had proclaimed his love to his wife two days ago not far from this very spot. Tears burned the back of her eyes. What a waste of a life. He'd appeared healthy the times she'd seen him.

"Was it a heart attack?" she asked Dr. Porter.

"No." Ryan said with conviction.

"How do you know?" She watched him.

"Yes, why don't you think it was a heart attack?" Dr. Porter, placed the instrument in the case and stood.

"He had jumpy eyes. You're his doctor. Did he have heart problems?" Ryan ran a hand across the back of his neck.

Shandra had learned he did that when he was stumped or baffled.

"No. Red Hasting is, or was healthy." Dr. Porter

stared at the man at their feet. "Stay with him while I get a gurney."

Ryan nodded.

Shandra moved closer to Ryan. She needed a hug. He put his arm around her, drawing her tight against him. She savored the beat of his heart and heat of his body.

Life.

She needed that after watching the man at their feet lose his.

Rumbling of small rubber tires announced Dr. Porter's approach. She moved out of Ryan's embrace. Along with the doctor and the gurney the antiseptic scent of the emergency room wafted out the open doors.

Ryan helped Dr. Porter lift the body onto the gurney.

"You going to tell his wife?" Dr. Porter asked.

"Yes. After I go talk to someone." Ryan glanced up and down the quiet street. "I don't think anyone will tell her before I do."

He grasped Shandra's elbow. "Come on. We have someone to talk to before I get you home and give Mrs. Hasting the bad news."

Shandra climbed into the Tahoe. "Where are we going?"

"Maxie's. Someone there put something in Hasting's drink." Ryan had a determined set to his jaw.

They drove the two blocks to Maxie's. She'd been in the bar on several occasions with Ted and Naomi. The establishment was the trendiest of the bars in town. The lighting wasn't as dim as the other bars and the clientele were local business persons or tourists. The other bars catered to the locals who liked to drink beer and gamble. Maxie's had mixed drinks and high-priced wines along with micro-brew beers.

Ryan parked on Pine Street. They walked around the corner to the entrance of the bar. Inside the doors, Ryan stopped and surveyed the clientele. "You know anyone in here?" he asked.

Shandra smiled. "The bartender and owner, Maxine." She sauntered up to the bar and took a seat in the middle of the bar close to the cash register, taps, and bottles. Maxine was at the end serving drinks to two men about forty.

"You know the bartender?" Ryan took the seat next to her.

"Ted and Naomi like to meet artists here. I've been in here several times with them." She smiled at him. "You'll like Maxine."

The woman glanced up, saw them, and smiled. Her long legs clad in skinny jeans brought her to a stop in front of them. She placed a coaster in front of Shandra and poured her favorite white wine. "What would you like, handsome?" Maxine askcd Ryan, fluttering her long, dark, fake lashes at him. Her strawberry blonde hair was piled on her head in a haphazard way, revealing her thin shoulders barely holding the peasant top over her double D breasts.

"Water and answers." He flashed his badge.

Maxine pouted as she stared at Shandra. "Doll, why'd you have to bring Debbie Downer to the party?"

Shandra laughed. "Sorry." Then she sobered. "Your answers could solve why a man died in my arms tonight."

"Oh my! I'm so sorry. Here let me give you

something stronger than fermented grape juice."

Maxine spun around, grabbed a bottle and a jigger. She poured whiskey into the jigger and placed it in front of Shandra. "That should help, Doll."

Maxine shifted her attention to Ryan, leaning onto her forearms and resting her plentiful bosom on the counter in front of him.

Shandra enjoyed watching men's reactions to the bar owner. She was curious how Ryan would react. To her relief he behaved as she'd hoped.

Ryan leaned back, opened his notepad, and directed his gaze to the woman's eyes and not her chest. "Did you see Red Hasting in here this evening?"

"Yes." Her head pivoted Shandra's direction. "Is that who died?"

Shandra nodded.

"Maxine, keep this to yourself. I still have to notify his next of kin." Ryan captured the woman's attention.

"That should have been easy. He was in here with June. They sat at the table in the corner." She pointed to the table near the hall to the restrooms.

"Did they leave together?" Ryan asked.

Maxine chewed on her narrow bottom lip. "I don't remember seeing either of them leave. I know June went to the restroom."

"What did Red have to drink? Did you wash the glass?" Ryan's gaze was fixed on a stack of dirty glasses sitting next to the sink.

"He had his usual whiskey and water." She glanced at the stacked dirty glasses. "One of those tumblers could be his." Her eyes narrowed. "You're going to take all of them, aren't you?"

Ryan stood. "I'm afraid so." He handed Shandra

the keys to his Tahoe. "Would you go grab my backpack out of the back of my vehicle?"

Shandra took the keys. "Yes." She left as Ryan rounded the bar and studied the pile of glasses.

Out on the sidewalk, she glanced up and down the side street. For the dozen or so people in the place there weren't that many vehicles parked. What had Red and June drove to town? Why did June leave him? She walked around the corner and stopped. A dull gray pickup slowly cruised by. Shandra pivoted on her heel to watch it move into the street light on Huckleberry. June sat behind the wheel of the pickup she'd parked by the clinic the other day. Why was she cruising? Was she looking for her husband or trying to find out if anyone had found him?

~*~

Ryan counted the glasses waiting on the drain board. "Which table did you say they were sitting at?" he asked Maxine. For a thin woman she had a large bust. Between the ample bust and the wad of hair on her head, she looked like two marshmallows on a stick.

She led him over to a table on the wall to the left of the bar.

"Thanks. Don't touch or add glasses to the pile by the sink. I'll bag them when Shandra brings in my kit."

She nodded and hustled back to the bar.

He should have asked if anyone else had sat here since the Hastings. He noticed a powdery substance on the table.

Shandra strode through the door. Her cheeks were rosy. "I saw June. She drove by slow in that pickup she was driving the other day."

Ryan pulled out his phone. He dialed Huckleberry dispatch. "Millie, it's Detective Greer. Send out the officer on duty. Have him pick up June Hasting. She's driving around in a pickup. Look up the plate number."

"Should she be treated as a suspect?" Millie asked.

"No. We need to tell her that her husband is dead."

"Does it have anything to do with the case you're working?" Millie asked.

"I can't say for sure until I talk with June. But my gut says it does." Ryan pushed the off button and held out a hand for his backpack.

Shandra handed it over. "What can I do?"

He nodded to the restrooms. "See if someone could sneak in or out of here that way."

She nodded and headed toward the restrooms.

Ryan brushed a sample of the powder into a small evidence bag with a brush from his evidence kit. He taped the bag closed with red evidence tape and noted where it was found, when, and the case number. Tucking the evidence into his backpack, he called Maxine over.

"The substance I cleaned off the table could be lethal. Clean it up and make sure no one else comes in contact with it."

The owner glared at him, but grabbed a wet rag and set to work cleaning up the table.

Ryan slipped behind the bar and bagged the tumbler-sized glasses.

Shandra returned. "Just past the men's room there is an office and a storage room to the left. The hallway ends, but the storage room door is open and it has an outside door to the alley."

Maxine strolled over. "You about through? My

customers are asking what you're doing."

"How many people know there's a way out of here through your storage room?" Ryan asked, zipping his bag shut.

"Are you thinking someone went in and out of here through my storage area? I better count my bottles." She spun as if to walk down the hallway.

Ryan caught her narrow wrist, keeping her attention. "Who knows about the door to the alley?"

"If you're asking does June. She does. She worked for me before she married Red."

Chapter Twenty-five

Shandra sat in the Huckleberry Police Station while Ryan called in warrants to search the Hasting house, vehicles, and even the Randal premise. The hands of the clock on the station wall ticked their way to straight-up midnight.

"Would you like a cup of coffee?" A woman a decade or so younger than Hazel asked from behind the partition of the dispatch area.

"No. I'd rather fall right to sleep when I get home." Shandra stood and walked over to the waist-high partition the woman sat behind. "How long do you think Ryan will be? I'll crash in his Tahoe if it looks like it could be a while."

"He shouldn't be long. He's writing up affidavits to get warrants." The woman leaned forward. "Did you and Ryan have a good time at his brother's wedding?"

Shandra smiled at the woman. "I suppose Hazel told you about the wedding?" She held out her hand.

"Shandra Higheagle."

"Millie Hamby. Pleased to meet you. It's protocol for everyone to know what the cop on a case is doing until the case is closed."

So this woman was Hazel's counterpart. Just as nosy too. "It was fine. I think it was good for Ryan to hang out with his family. He works too hard."

"That he does. But when you're a large area with small police forces, you make do." Millie sipped from a steaming mug she picked up off her desk.

Shandra had a question that had been bugging her. "Since Ryan has to go officially tell June her husband is dead, why doesn't he just do that and ask the questions I know he wants to ask?"

"Because without a warrant in his hand, if she refuses to answer his questions, he won't be able to search her house and look for whatever killed her husband. She could toss him out and then get rid of the evidence." Millie half shut one eye. "If you're going to hang around with Ryan, you'll have to study up on the correct way to do things. From what I hear you tend to do things that could get you killed."

Shandra's cheeks heated from embarrassment. It just made more sense to tackle the problem head on than have to jump through hoops. The woman insinuating she was a loose cannon only made her more intent on finding the truth.

A door opened and Ryan walked out. He stopped at Millie's desk. "There should be warrants coming over the fax. When Deputy Trapp gets here, give them to him and tell him and the other deputies to meet me at June Hasting's house."

"Will do. Good luck." Millie picked up her cup and took a drink.

Ryan exited the area and motioned to the door. "I'll drop you off on my way to the Hasting house."

Shandra waited until they were in the vehicle and out of earshot of anyone. "I'd rather go to the house with you. If we're wrong about June killing her husband, and possibly J.W., she'll need someone."

Ryan stared at her before starting the engine. "If she did kill her husband, and I'm assuming it was to hide her involvement with Randal's death, she is a dangerous person. I'd rather you were tucked in your bed away from any danger." He started the vehicle and backed away from the curb.

"If you bring me along to tell her about her husband, she isn't going to know we suspect her." Shandra wasn't going to let Ryan walk up to the Hasting house alone. If the woman was crazy enough to kill her husband, who know what she'd do to a lone policeman.

Ryan didn't say anything as he drove fast out of town with his lights flashing.

Shandra settled back in the seat. Arguing with him wouldn't work. They both had opposing views of the situation.

Ryan's phone beeped. He pulled the phone out of the case on his hip. "Greer."

She peered at him through the darkness in the cab. The road had little traffic during the day and even less at night. She couldn't rely on the headlights of oncoming cars to see his reactions to the phone call.

"What do you mean the judge refuses to sign the warrant? I gave clear justification for the need." Ryan swore under his breath and shoved the phone into the case.

Shandra waited. He needed time to rethink.

Ryan flicked off the flashing lights but continued down the county road at sixty. Damn. He'd wanted that warrant so he could search the house and grounds.

Shandra shifted in the seat next to him.

Her road was coming up. He had to make a decision. Drop her off at home where he knew she'd be safe, or take her along to help smoke out the truth.

He grit his teeth. Without a warrant he'd need Shandra. He kept the accelerator on sixty and rushed by her driveway.

She let out a loud whoosh of air.

"I don't like this, but I'm going to need your help since the warrants didn't go through." His gut was twisting like it did the night he'd walked into an ambush in Chicago.

"I promise to do whatever you ask."

"At some point while I'm talking with June, excuse yourself to go to the bathroom. Look for drugs. I found a powdery substance on the table where they sat in Maxie's. I'm pretty sure when the autopsy comes in it will say Red was overdosed."

"Okay." Shandra leaned forward.

"What are you doing?" He couldn't take his eyes off the road for very long at this speed. There could be animals or potholes that would throw them over the edge.

"Getting my phone out of my purse. I'll take photos of the prescription drugs I find."

"Good idea." He braked for the Randal's driveway.

The gates were still closed. He stopped and Shandra opened her door.

"I can—" he started to say.

"I grew up on a ranch. I know how to open and close a gate." The humor in her voice made him smile.

"Leave the gate open."

She nodded in the beam of the headlights.

Back in the vehicle she asked, "Do you think June is home?"

"The officer on patrol didn't see her vehicle in Huckleberry. I think after she did her cruise by she came home and is waiting for someone to show up." He pointed to the dark main house and the downstairs light on in the cabin on the far side of the barn.

He drove up to the walkway that led to the front door, killed the lights, and studied the windows. A curtain on the window with the light moved slightly.

"She's awake. Let's see how she answers the door." Ryan checked his holster. A habit that got him searched every time he'd encountered the gang leaders.

He waited for Shandra to exit and catch up to him before he walked up to the front door. He wanted to know where she was at all times. It was the only way to keep her safe.

He rapped on the door three times and waited.

Rapid footsteps followed by the door swinging wide revealed June Hasting dressed in pajamas, her hair in a braid. "Red?" she questioned. Then stepped back when her gaze landed on Ryan and then Shandra.

"Detective, Miss Higheagle, what are you doing here?" She put a hand to her mouth. "Is it Red? I knew something was wrong."

Ryan grasped the woman's arm, guiding her into

the small, but cozily furnished home.

"What did you know was wrong?" Ryan asked, easing the woman onto a chair. He took the sofa. Shandra wandered off toward what appeared to be the kitchen.

"When I came out of the restroom at Maxie's, Red was gone. I'd told him I'd only be a few minutes. But he must have been so upset with me he didn't wait." She hiccupped. Tears glistened in her eyes.

"Here." Shandra placed a glass of water in the woman's hands.

"How long were you in the restroom?" Ryan asked, not believing a bit of the story or the theatrics. He knew when someone was genuinely upset and when they were faking.

"I don't know. Five minutes, maybe. I had to wait for a stall." She dabbed at her eyes with the sleeve of her pajamas.

"What were you fighting about?" Ryan asked. He wanted to pull out his notepad, but that would look like he was interrogating her. Which he was and didn't want her to know.

Her head jerked, and her brown eyes narrowed. "It doesn't matter. Why are you here?"

"Your husband died outside the Emergency Care Center tonight." He wasn't going to sugar coat the news. He had a feeling she already knew.

"No!" she wailed and flung her body over the arm of the chair.

Ryan glanced at Shandra. She wasn't buying the woman's theatrics either from the frown on her face.

"Would you like us to call someone to come be

with you?" Shandra asked.

"I have no one," the woman wailed.

"Surely, Vivian or Cecily?" Shandra persisted.

"Those bitches would only laugh."

Shandra's eyes widened in shock as her gaze met Ryan's.

He nodded for her to go search the bathrooms. Shandra silently disappeared from the room.

"Mrs. Hasting, what were you and your husband doing in town tonight?" Ryan pulled his notepad out. He was pretty sure he was investigating a homicide, and the woman in front of him was his best suspect.

She sat up, sniffed, and drug her pajama sleeve under her nose. "We needed a night out. All that has been happening this week. We needed a change."

"But we saw you out earlier in the week. You were eating at the Italian restaurant." He waited a beat. When she didn't say anything, he added, "Shandra and I saw you and Red arguing in the street by the clinic after we left the restaurant that night."

Her back straightened, and her gaze locked onto him. "We weren't…How did you…" She closed her mouth and stared at him.

He could tell her mind was clicking to find the right lie even though her eyes were blank. What was she going to make up?

"You haven't even asked how your husband died." He'd flip topics. The more he kept her mind buzzing the more likely she'd slip up with a lie.

"H-how did he die?" she asked, but she turned her head as if she really didn't want to know.

"From what Dr. Porter could tell, he suffocated and had cardiac arrest. Did your husband have a history of heart or breathing problems?"

"Yes. He did. His heart—"

"Who's your doctor?" he interrupted to throw her off the lie she was about to spew.

"Dr. Porter. He's the only one in town."

"He said your husband had no history of heart problems." He'd caught her.

And she knew it.

June sputtered and started to stand.

Ryan put a hand out, restraining her. "Where are you going?"

"I-I…" Her gaze landed on the almost empty glass. "I was going to get more water."

"I'll get that for you." Ryan picked up the glass. Where was Shandra? She should have returned by now.

"Down the hall," June called out behind him.

Shandra ducked into the bedroom closet when she heard June scurrying down the hall to the bedroom. She had a good idea what the woman planned to do. She'd photographed a nearly empty bottle of anxiety pills in the medicine cabinet. Pills that had been prescribed this week. The day she visited the clinic. There was no way the bottle should be that empty.

June ran across the room to the bathroom and grabbed the bottle. She struggled with the lid while standing in front of the toilet.

Shandra stepped out of the closet and clicked the camera on her phone.

June spun around with the bottle in her hands, her mouth wide open.

Shandra clicked another photo.

"You!" June shrieked and launched at Shandra.

Shandra tossed her phone on the bed and shoved the crazed woman to the ground.

June crawled to her hands and knees and leaped at Shandra. The woman moved so fast. Shandra was unprepared for the hit. The woman shoved her head into Shandra's stomach and a fist connected with her cheek.

The last time she'd been struck, she'd froze. And been the victim of more injuries. She pummeled the woman's head and kicked her off. They both shot to their feet.

Her mind flashed to the core move she'd learned at the self-defense classes she'd taken after Carl threatened her.

June sprang at her again.

Shandra used the woman's momentum to tumble her to the ground on her stomach. Before June could gain her breath, Shandra sat on her back, pulling June's arms behind her.

"Shandra, careful she's pregnant," Ryan said, bursting through the door.

"No, she's not. It was just another one of her lies." Shandra held June's arms until Ryan slipped handcuffs on her. "While I was digging around for evidence of the drug used to kill her husband, I found a current prescription of birth control pills with five pills missing and a clear bag with different types of pregnancy testers. They have been altered to look like a positive test."

"You're as nosy as those two bitches next door." June raised her head off the carpet and glared at Shandra.

"What happened? Did your husband discover you weren't pregnant? Did you need to silence him from saying you were the one who went hunting in the woods with Randal and only you came back?" Ryan pulled the woman to her feet.

The mousy woman who hid behind her husband the day Shandra visited the Randal house was gone. In her place was a strong, confident, psychopath.

June laughed. "I didn't pull the trigger, Red did. I told him I was pregnant with J.W.'s baby and he'd found out. That J.W. planned to take the baby and not let me see it when it was born."

"Why did you want J.W. dead?" Shandra asked, touching her throbbing cheek before scooping her phone off the bed.

"He told me he was going to leave Vivian. He said I was more woman than he'd ever need." Her eyes darkened and her lips curled into a sneer. "Then I saw his hands all over Cecily one night and later caught him out in the woods with his hands all over some young girl." Tears slid down her cheeks. "He'd used me just like he used everyone in his life. He thought bringing in help would appease me. I didn't want help with my work. I wanted him. When I faked the pregnancy, hoping to get him to commit to me, he laughed. Laughed! Said Red should be happy he'd finally have a brat.

"I was taking a walk in the woods when I spotted him with the young girl again. At first, I wanted to run up and kill them both. But I noticed he was being too precise about how the girl stood, and that he kept her face turned to him. That's when I realized he was using the wildlife camera he'd set up there to photograph their actions." She wiped at the tears and crossed her arms. "I didn't understand it all. After he posed with the girl in provocative poses, her half-dressed, he told her to dress and sent her away. I followed the girl. She tried to ignore me when I stopped her by her car on the old logging road. I made a grab for her coat and came up with the necklace. The one J.W. had so expertly waved in front of the camera.

"She drove off. I told Red that J.W. was using the cameras to photograph his sexual exploits with minors." She laughed. "That set him off. He hated the way J.W. did the illegal hunting and following the animals with all his cameras. Red said he was going to turn him in to Fish and Game."

"That doesn't make sense." Shandra interrupted. Ryan frowned at her.

"Why would J.W. make that tape with Clower's daughter before the investigation started?"

"Clower had been sniffing around here before Red called it in. I think he already knew about the illegal hunting. Or his daughter." June shook the cuffs holding her hands. "I gotta go pee. Could you take these off?"

Ryan shook his head. "I'm not letting you loose. You can use the facilities at the county jail." He moved the woman ahead of him down the hall. "Shandra come with me. I'll need your help."

Shandra slipped her phone into her back pocket and followed them out to the Tahoe.

"I'm going to buckle her in the back seat and call for backup. Then I'll go back in. I need to take photos and collect evidence." Ryan stopped beside the vehicle and opened the back door.

"Want me to move our stuff out of the back?" Shandra asked, moving to the opposite side of the vehicle.

"No, she's…Oooof!"

Shandra's stomach churned at the sound of something snapping.

She rounded the vehicle.

Ryan lay on the ground gasping for air. A streak of white flashed through the trees as June dashed into the forest.

Chapter Twenty-six

Sirens and lights made Ryan's head throb even more. He'd been damn stupid to not treat that woman like a violent suspect. He'd been distracted, thinking about collecting evidence. She'd jammed both her feet into his chest, cracking the ribs on his left side. The force of the blow sent him backwards, smacking his head on the ground, hard.

Sitting on the tailgate of a search and rescue truck, he sucked air through his clenched teeth. Pain speared his chest with each breath.

"You have a couple fractured ribs," the search and rescue medic said, putting tape over the area that burned with each breath he took.

"You have any idea where she's headed?" Sheriff Oldham asked.

"No. She's crazy I can tell you that. Anyone out in those woods looking for her needs to be alert and armed." Pain radiated through his chest with each breath and movement. Talking was the last thing he wanted to do, but he had to make sure everyone looking for the woman knew how wily she was.

"Check all the buildings. She could circle back and hide." Searing pain radiated in his chest. "She's handcuffed. That should slow her down."

"We've checked all the buildings and have people watching them in case she does try to slip back and get her things." Oldham put a hand on his shoulder. "Miss Higheagle said she would drive you to her place to rest while we expand the search."

"I'm going to help you search." Ryan stood. Nausea swirled bile to his throat. His increased breathing increased the pain and added to the throbbing in his head. He dropped back to the tailgate.

"Take it slow and easy." The medic held out a hand with two pills and a bottle of water in his other hand. "Take these to lessen the pain so you can breathe."

Ryan swallowed the pills.

"You're no good to us. The medic said you need to take it easy. You can't be traipsing around in the forest." Sheriff Oldham put an arm under Ryan's. "I'll put you in your vehicle. Miss Higheagle will take you to her house. I'll keep you informed about the search."

Ryan nodded and tried not to inhale deeply as the sheriff slowly maneuvered him to the passenger side of the Tahoe.

"Lil and I can get him out of the vehicle and into the house, sheriff." Shandra's voice was a welcome sound. If she drove him to her house, he could keep an eye on her as she nursed him.

Shandra's chest constricted as she studied Ryan. She'd never seen his complexion so pale. His face was pinched with pain.

"Can you fish the keys out of your pant pocket or do I need to try?" she asked.

Ryan slowly moved his hand toward his left pant pocket. 'I can't." He drew in a short breath. "Same side as…"

"I'll get them." Her hand hesitated twice as she leaned over him to reach into the warmth of his pocket to fish the keys out.

He remained with his head resting against the back of the seat, his eyes closed. She didn't know if it was from pain or he was savoring her hand in his pants. Her heart raced as her fingers moved deeper into his pocket before touching the warm metal.

"Got 'em." She backed away and closed the door before walking to the driver's side. She climbed in and carefully set the car in motion down the Randal's driveway.

She'd bet more than the pain inflicted by the woman had Ryan so quiet. He'd lost a suspect after she'd confessed. Letting a woman get the better of him had to be part of his silence and pain. Seeing him in pain, tugged at maternal urges she hadn't known she possessed.

"I don't understand why June killed Red like she did. There was no one else who could have given him the drugs. She set herself up to be caught." Shandra glanced over at Ryan. "It doesn't make sense."

"Maybe after getting Red to do the first killing she thought she wouldn't get caught." Ryan's breathy reply barely carried across the cab to her.

She turned onto the county road and then turned up her drive. "I'm going to go slow, but you may need to grit your teeth. You know how bumpy this road is."

Creeping up her driveway, Shandra had a premonition they would see June soon. It would make sense for her to come to Shandra's to get food, clothing, or even a horse. She was the closest full-time neighbor. June could hole up in some of the summer houses that were closer to town, but she'd need transportation to get there. Walking would take her a couple days.

Shandra parked as close to the front door as she could get. "I'm going to get Lil to help me move you into the house."

Ryan started to protest.

"Stay put. I'll only be a minute." Shandra slipped out of the vehicle and headed to the barn. She could have entered the back door closest to the tack room where Lil stayed. Instead, knowing June could be hiding in the trees behind the buildings, she opted to use the door at the front of the barn. She wasn't going to make it easy for the woman if she was lurking about. Touching her bruised cheek, she vowed to not let the woman get the better of her again.

The front door opened silently. Lil maintained all the working parts of the ranch. No hinge squeaked whether it was a door, window, or gate. Shandra slid sideways through a narrow gap. The light was on under Lil's door.

Why hasn't Sheba detected me by now? The dog had good hearing. Her sense of smell also detected things before Shandra saw or heard anything. She walked softly to the tack room door. Sheba's frightened whimper came from the room.

She calculated the distance from here to June's

house. They had been delayed at the Randal's for nearly two hours. She could have made a straight line to here.

Centimeter by centimeter, Shandra turned the knob on the tack room door. Then eased the door open a fraction at a time. If June was holding Sheba and Lil hostage, she didn't want them to come to harm. Peeking through the crack in the door, she spotted Sheba cowering under the bed and Lil tied up on the bed.

She eased the door open more. They were alone. She slipped in. Sheba crawled out from under the bed whimpering. "Shhhh. We don't know the mean person is gone," Shandra whispered as she ungagged and untied Lil.

"How long ago did she do this?" Shandra asked, tossing the ropes on the ground.

"About fifteen or twenty minutes ago. I heard some banging behind the studio. I went to look and found her breaking the chains on the handcuffs. Before I made sense of the situation, she had me hogtied." Lil stood and dug under the mattress. She came up with two handguns. "She took my shotgun and one of the horses. The rhythm of the hooves sounded like Apple."

Lil headed to the door.

"We have to get Ryan into the house and call the search party. They started at the Randal's, but they're a good hour behind if they're headed this way through the woods."

"Leave the detective. He ain't any worse off than sitting in the house knowing we're following her." She grabbed a saddle bag slung over a hook. "Come on. You can call the sheriff while we follow her."

"The woman is crazy. We're crazy to go out there after her." Shandra grasped Lil's arm.

Lil's gaze scanned her face. "I see she unleashed on you already." She peered into Shandra's eyes. "I have to go after her. She took my daddy's shot gun. Poppa gave it to me a year after Momma and Daddy died. He told me as long as I had it I'd always have a piece of my daddy with me."

Shandra wasn't sure she wanted to follow a crazy woman with a shot gun. She knew what the woman was capable of without a gun. But if she didn't go, she knew Lil would go by herself.

"I'll call the sheriff while you saddle the horses." Shandra went outside and walked to the Tahoe.

Ryan would have the sheriff's number on his phone. The problem would be explaining why she needed it and keeping him in the vehicle.

She opened the door. Ryan barely moved, but his hands started to unbuckle the seat belt.

"No. Stay buckled." She put her hands over his. "I need your phone to call the sheriff."

"Why?" he asked, opening his eyes, and peering into hers. The pain killers the medic gave him made his eyes dull and glassy.

"Lil thinks she spotted June going by here. I want to let him know." It was a bit of a lie but if she told him the truth he'd try to stop her.

"We need to get inside and lock the doors." Ryan's hands moved to the seatbelt again.

"We will. Relax. I'm going to close the door and make the call." She slipped his phone from his belt and closed the vehicle door. Within seconds she found the Sheriff's number.

"Greer, what are you doing calling me?" The man's

voice was gruff.

"Sir, it's Shandra. I returned to my place and found my employee tied up. June's been here and took one of my horses. Lil and I are going to follow her."

"No you're not. Where's Greer? I want to speak to him."

"He doesn't know what I'm doing. I'm taking his phone so you can track me. Don't call. June has a shot gun." She clicked the phone off and headed to the barn.

Lil had Sunshine and Duke saddled and ready to go.

"Where's Sheba?" Shandra asked, looking for her dog.

"I thought it best to lock her in my room. She was shaken up. We don't need her stumbling into June and getting shot." Lil swung onto her horse. "I found her tracks. Looks like she's headed back through the Randal property."

Chapter Twenty-seven

Ryan shook his head to clear the fog the pain killers made in his brain. What he couldn't figure out was why it was taking Shandra so long to get back here and help him into the house and why she hadn't brought his phone back. Knowing he let a dangerous killer get away didn't help his situation.

After several tries, his eyes finally focused on his watch. Four forty-five. No wonder the sky was growing lighter. Where the hell was Shandra? He fumbled with the seat buckle and shoved the door open. The shockwaves of his feet hitting the ground reverberated through his ribs, causing a round of nausea. He stood next to the vehicle, waiting for the nausea and pain to subside.

One slow step in front of the other took him to the front door. It wasn't locked. She must have went inside to get something and maybe sat down and fell asleep. He knew she was beat when they left the police station.

Calling out wasn't an option. His ribs wouldn't take that much volume of air in his lungs.

After a slow search he was positive she wasn't in the house. He shuffled to the phone in the kitchen and dialed Sheriff Oldham's number. The phone went to voice-mail.

"Sheriff, this is Greer. I can't find Shandra. She used my phone to call you, what is going on?" He replaced the phone, drew in several short breaths, and made his way to the back door. He'd find Lil. She knew Shandra's every move.

~*~

Shandra let Lil lead. She didn't like having her friend in the front, but Lil knew how to track. The sky was brightening and the air grew colder. She shivered and huddled down into a more compact space. *I should have grabbed another coat to go over this one.* She had on her traveling jacket not her thick coat she usually wore when riding in the forest.

Lil didn't appear cold. She leaned over, peering at the ground. Her winter shearling coat would keep her warm. She held up a hand and slid off her horse.

Shandra dismounted and walked carefully up to Lil. "What is it?" she whispered.

"I think she stopped." Lil whispered back. "Hold the horses and I'll take a closer look."

Shandra grabbed the woman's arm. "Don't. If we stay put the search party will find us and her."

"I don't take kindly to being tied up." Lil glared into the trees.

"I know, but I don't want you hurt. She's already killed a person and assaulted a policeman." Shandra held onto Lil. "Let's just wait a bit and see what she does."

Lil nodded. But her gaze remained riveted to a spot in the trees Shandra couldn't see.

They waited ten minutes. Shandra stood beside Duke. Leaning against Duke, using the stirrup as an anchor, she closed her tired, stinging eyes.

Ella tapped her on the shoulder. She is coming and so is help, she whispered.

Duke snorted, but it was June's voice asking, "How did you get loose?" that jolted Shandra's eyes open.

The woman had her back to the horses, the shotgun pointed at Lil's back. The chain on the handcuffs dangled from her wrists.

Shandra stood behind the two horses who were side by side. Apparently, it wasn't light enough for June to see two horses.

She could send the horses running, but startling June could cause her to pull the trigger.

There had to be a way to keep her busy until help arrived.

"Where do you plan to hide?" Shandra asked, ducking behind the horses.

"Who's there? Get out here or I'll shoot Crazy Lil." June's tone was hesitant.

"How do you know I don't have a gun on you?" Shandra recalled the two pistols Lil had dug out from under the mattress. She'd had one in her hand earlier and knowing Lil, she probably put the other one in Shandra's saddle bag.

"If you had a gun you would have used it by now." Again June's voice didn't sound convinced.

Shandra carefully felt the outside of the saddlebag

on her side of Duke. Yep. The outline of a handgun pressed against her fingers. The next problem was getting to it and making sure no person or animal was shot on the process.

With slow movements, she unbuckled the flap on the saddlebag and slid her hand under the flap, grasping the handle of the gun.

A horse snorted deeper in the forest. That would have to be Apple. A good diversion.

Shandra whistled for Apple.

He nickered. The sound of hooves echoed along the forest floor.

"What—" June's voice fell away.

Shandra ducked under the horse's necks and pushed the barrel of the pistol against June's back.

Apple burst through the trees and dug in his haunches to stop.

June screeched, pointing the shotgun toward the horse.

Lil grabbed the shotgun.

Boom! The blast echoed through the trees. Before the sound died, pellets rained down around them.

Shandra dropped the pistol, stuck out a leg, and grabbed June's hair, tripping the woman to the ground. June's arms were flailing as Shandra fell on top of her. Another blow landed on her already bruised cheek.

Shandra growled as she tried to contain the woman.

June wriggled, swung her fists backwards, and tried to bring her legs up underneath her. Shandra pressed her weight down on the woman, knocking her legs out from under her when she tried to get to her knees.

Another shot gun blast boomed.

June paused momentarily. Lil planted her knees in the woman's back and helped pull June's arms behind her.

People in uniforms came running, leaping through the underbrush.

Male hands came into view. They captured June's hands, clicking handcuffs around her wrists next to Ryan's handcuffs. Shandra and Lil were pulled to their feet and someone dragged June to her feet.

"Miss Higheagle that was a foolish thing to do," scolded Deputy Speaks.

"She had a gun on Lil." Shandra wrapped her arms around the woman holding the shotgun and glaring at June.

Chapter Twenty-eight

Ryan leaned against the side of the barn. His muddled head and the piercing pain in his ribs made searching the premise slow. But he had a bad feeling. Sunshine, Apple, and Duke were all missing from the corral.

Barking and talking made him spin away from the corral fence. The action added to the pain twinging in his side.

"Ryan! Ryan where are you?" Shandra's voice drifted to him.

He wanted to reply but held back knowing it would bring on another round of excruciating pain.

He waited.

Sheba bounded into sight, barking. She stopped just short of knocking him down and licked his hand.

Shandra ran to his side. "What are you doing out here?" Her arms wrapped around him, drawing his body away from the rough wood wall.

"Looking for you. Where have you been?" He

stared at her in the growing light of dawn.

The sound of footsteps drew his gaze away from the stubborn woman. Sheriff Oldham, Speaks, and Lil were behind her.

"You should be in bed." Shandra kissed his forehead.

He stared closely at her. "Why do you have pine needles in your hair? And your face? What or should I say who put that bruise on your cheek?"

"Help me get him into bed," she said to the sheriff and deputy. "When you're comfortable," she said to Ryan, "I'll tell you what happened."

Ryan had a feeling he wasn't going to like what he heard. He gave in, knowing she wouldn't tell him a thing until she deemed him comfortable. The men helped him into the house, undressed him down to his underwear, and eased him into the guest bed.

"Where did Shandra go? Was she in danger?" he asked.

"You'll have to wait for her to tell you. Not my business," Sheriff Oldham said. "But I can tell you, we brought in Melvin Clower and questioned him about the necklace and his daughter. J.W. Randal had been using Clower's daughter to try and blackmail Clower into not taking the illegal hunting violations to court. Clower shipped his wife and daughter off to his sister in California to keep the man from using his family as leverage. Randal had threatened the Clower girl to get her to pose for the photos on the wildlife camera. Clower found them before Randal had a chance to try and blackmail him."

Once Ryan was covered, they called Shandra and

Lil into the room.

"I'm guessing from the stalling, I'm not going to like what you have to say." He glanced from his superior, to the deputy, then to Lil. They all kept their gazes on Shandra.

She picked up his hand, cleared her throat, and told him about chasing after June.

Ryan squeezed her hand when she told about taking the pistol out of the saddlebag and confronting June.

"You could have been killed. What were you thinking?" His insides curdled at the thought of June shooting her with the shotgun.

"All I could think of was making sure no one got hurt until the search team arrived." She squeezed his hand. "I knew help was close."

He understood her meaning. Her grandmother had told her. But that didn't make what she did settle any easier in his gut.

"When you're up to it we need both your statements about what happened at the house before Mrs. Hasting got away." Sheriff Oldham nodded to Shandra. "Miss Higheagle said the woman confessed to getting her husband to kill J.W. and to killing her husband."

"Yes. Mrs. Hasting is a dangerous woman." Ryan gingerly touched the bruise on Shandra's face. "I should have never underestimated her aggressiveness."

"Miss Higheagle, make sure he sees a doctor and is cleared before he comes back to work," Sheriff Oldham said, moving toward the door. "Ryan I don't want to see you in the office until your ribs have healed." The two men exited the room.

"I'll see them out and take care of the animals," Lil said, backing out of the room.

Shandra knew what she'd done had been foolish. But she'd do it again if someone she cared about was hell bent on chasing a psychopath. She brushed the hair off Ryan's forehead. "I know I took a risk riding after June. But she'd tied Lil up and took her daddy's shotgun. Lil was out for revenge. She would have ridden off by herself if I hadn't gone with her." She sat on the side of the bed. "We weren't alone. Grandmother told me June was coming and help would be there soon. I knew I just had to make sure she didn't kill Lil before help came."

Ryan peered into her eyes. "I know you are never alone. Your grandmother watches over you, but Shandra, you aren't invincible. No one is."

"I know." Her father came to mind. She had vague memories of riding on his shoulders and feeling safe even though she was high in the air. She studied Ryan's face. She also felt safe when he was around. And he'd be around for a while if she allowed her heart to open and let him in.

Nursing Ryan would be a good chance for her to see if he had a Jekyll Hyde persona like the last man she'd fallen for. Having Ryan around would also give her a chance to bounce around some of the things she'd found out so far about her father's death. He might have some ideas of where else she could look for information.

Once Ryan was well, she planned to dig into her father's death as if it had just happened.

~*~

About the Author

Paty Jager is an award-winning author of 50+ novels, 10 novellas, and numerous anthologies of murder mystery and western romance. All her work has Western or Native American elements in them along with hints of humor and engaging characters. Paty and her husband raise alfalfa hay in rural eastern Oregon. Riding horses and battling rattlesnakes, she not only writes the western lifestyle, she lives it.

This is what Mysteries Etc says about her Shandra Higheagle mystery series: "Mystery, romance, small town, and Native American heritage combine to make a compelling read."

You can purchase print books from Paty's website; https://www.patyjager.net and you can also sign up for her newsletter (https://bit.ly/2IhmWcm) where you learn about her life, what she's writing, specials, and where she'll be at in-person events. You also get a puzzle every month to solve.

If you enjoy the Shandra Higheagle series, please leave a review at Bookbub, Goodreads, the store where you purchased the book, or tell your friends on social media and in person. A review is the best way to encourage a writer to continue writing more books.

Books in the Shandra Higheagle Mystery Series

Double Duplicity
Tarnished Remains
Deadly Aim
Murderous Secrets
Killer Descent
Reservation Revenge
Yuletide Slaying
Fatal Fall
Haunting Corpse
Argtful Murder
Dangerous Dance
Homicide Hideaway
Toxic Trigger-point
Abstract Casualty
Capricious Demise
Vanishing Dream
And a novella
Christmas Chaos

Thank you for purchasing this Windtree Press publication. For other books of the heart, please visit our website at www.windtreepress.com.

For questions or more information contact us at info@windtreepress.com.

Windtree Press
Corvallis, OR

www.windtreepress.com